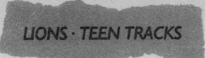

Phoebe

How could her best friends act like such jerks, Phoebe wondered furiously as she walked home from the pool. Pretending to drown to get a lifeguard's attention – how idiotic could a person get? What had gotten into them? Her pace slowed as the heat of the midafternoon caused the sweat to pour down her. The hotter she got, the angrier she felt. How could three people change so much in two months? Her mother said it was natural, that it was all part of growing up. Well, if that was what growing up was all about, Phoebe had one response. No thanks.

The Sisters series by Marilyn Kaye

Phoebe
Daphne
Cassie
Lydia

Marilyn Kaye

Phoebe

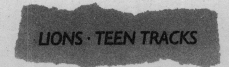

LIONS · TEEN TRACKS

First published in the USA 1987 by
Harcourt Brace Jovanovich, Publishers
First published in Great Britain 1988 by
Lions Teen Tracks

Lions Teen Tracks is an imprint of
the Children's Division, part of
the Collins Publishing Group,
8 Grafton Street, London W1X 3LA

Printed and bound in Great Britain by
William Collins Sons & Co. Ltd, Glasgow

For the memory of my mother, Annette Rudman Kaye

1

"Eighty-nine girls at Camp Ne-Hoc,
Round the fire at twelve o'clock,
No one saw the falling rock,
Eighty-eight girls at Camp Ne-Hoc."

PHOEBE GRAY SANG ALONG lustily with the rest of the returning campers, but her face was pressed against the window. Way ahead, she could see a sign—if she didn't blink, she might be able to read it before the bus whizzed by.

"Chicago, twenty miles," she yelled out over "eighty-seven girls at Camp Ne-Hoc."

A scattered cheer went up from the crowd, but her seatmate brushed an imaginary tear from her eye.

"No more Ne-Hoc," she wailed. "Oh, Fee, I can't bear it."

Fee grinned at her. "Cheer up, Danielle. We'll be back in ten months. Besides, don't you want to see your mom?"

"Oh, sure," Danielle said. "I mean, I missed my mom and all that. It's just that after camp, home always seems so quiet and boring."

"You're kidding!" Fee exclaimed. "Boy, it's never quiet at my house."

Danielle looked at her enviously. "You're so lucky to have all those sisters."

Fee started to agree enthusiastically, but then remembered that Danielle was an only child with just a mother. She didn't want to make her feel worse.

"Look at it this way," she said. "At least you get your own room."

"Which one do you share with? Cassie?"

Fee shook her head. "No, it's me and Daphne. Cassie's with Lydia."

Danielle sighed wistfully. "It must be fun, a big family like that. Just like one of those TV shows."

Fee nodded happily. "It is, kind of, because we're all just one year apart. But we're all so different." She could have gone on and on, but Danielle had heard it all before in the cabin.

Her friend took over for her. "Let me see if I've got it all. Lydia's the oldest, right?"

"Right. She's fourteen."

"And Cassie's thirteen, and she's the pretty one. Daphne's twelve, and she's shy. What does she look like?"

Fee visualized her next-oldest sister. "She's about three inches taller than me, she's got dark straight hair, and has real dark eyes. She wears glasses and she's skinny."

"Then you guys don't look a bit alike, do you?"

Fee looked down at her own chunky body and fingered a strand of limp, light-brown hair. "Not a bit," she admitted. "Hey, you can see for yourself at the bus stop. I'll bet they'll all be there to meet me. Unless my mom stays home to fry chicken."

"How do you know you're going to have fried chicken?"

"Because it's my favorite food," Fee said complacently. "And she always makes my favorites when I come home from camp." She smiled dreamily. "We'll probably have double chocolate fudge cake for dessert, too."

Danielle began to look a little more cheerful. "My mom will make a big fuss too. And my two best friends will come over, and she'll take us all to Burger Monster."

Fee looked thoughtful. "I wonder if Mom invited Linn and Jessica and Melanie over for dinner. They're my best friends, and—"

"I know, I know," Danielle interrupted. "And you've been best friends since first grade, and you have a secret club with a secret language that nobody knows."

Danielle was grinning as she said this, but Fee went a little pink. Maybe she did talk about her family and her friends a lot. But there was so much to tell!

Danielle joined in on "fifty-six girls at Camp Ne-Hoc," but Fee closed her eyes and tried to imagine what everyone in her family was doing right that minute. Her mother might be frying the chicken, and her father was probably leaving his office as editor of the *Cedar*

3

Park Journal to pick up the family at home. Lydia would be dashing home from somewhere, late as usual. Daphne was certain to be in their room, reading or drawing or writing something. And Cassie would be in front of a mirror, pulling a brush through her long blonde hair.

Out the window, another sign caught her eye. Chicago—Next Exit. A happy shiver ran through her. In less than an hour she'd be entertaining her family with camp stories. She envisioned a rapt audience hanging onto every word, laughing at some stories, gasping at others. When she described the tricks they'd played on the counselors—frogs in their beds, salt in the sugar bowl—her mother would frown, but there'd be a twinkle in her eye. And her father would roar with laughter.

And after dinner, the gang would come over, and she'd go through all her stories again. And then maybe they'd play Monopoly, or write their pen pals. . . .

"Hey, Fee!"

With mild reluctance, Phoebe pushed aside her daydreams and turned again to Danielle.

"I heard a rumor that Ne-Hoc's going to start taking boys next summer."

Phoebe wrinkled her nose. "You're kidding! Yech!"

"Oh, I don't know," Danielle said thoughtfully. "Maybe it won't be so bad."

Boys? At camp? Phoebe thought it was a revolting idea.

Danielle sighed loudly. "I'm going to miss camp so much. I can't believe I'm not going to see you guys again for ten months."

"You know, we only live about an hour from each other," Phoebe reminded her.

Danielle nodded seriously. "That's true. And this year we're all going to get together, right?"

"Absolutely," Phoebe replied. She knew from experience that as they departed the bus, they'd all promise to write or call or meet during the school year. They wouldn't, though. Once they got home, they'd all get swept up into their own private worlds that had nothing to do with Camp Ne-Hoc. And even though she'd had a super time at camp, Phoebe couldn't wait to get back to her own private world.

The campers were now down to "forty-three girls at Camp Ne-Hoc," and Phoebe joined in. But as she sang, her mind drifted—to her friends, her parents, her sisters. Another sign was coming up, and she leaned over to catch it. Then she gathered her knees in her arms and curled up in happy anticipation.

The sign said Welcome to Chicago. But in her mind it read Welcome Home, Phoebe.

2

AN EAR-SHATTERING COMBINATION of cheers and applause filled the bus as they pulled into the parking lot. Up in front, a counselor was yelling, "Stay in your seats until the bus comes to a complete stop." No one paid any attention. Some kids had leaped across their seats to bang on the windows and wave. Others were jumping up and putting on knapsacks, gathering bags from under the seats, and yanking down suitcases from overhead racks.

From her window, Phoebe scanned the crowd in the parking lot for a glimpse of her parents and sisters. She thought she saw her father for a second, but then the bus turned away to park.

When it finally came to a complete stop, Phoebe leaped up to join the crush in the aisle. She pressed herself into the group of girls, surging toward the bus door inch by inch. "Fee, I'll call you," Danielle yelled.

"Okay," Phoebe called back, but already her bunkmates and Camp Ne-Hoc were fading from the present and dissolving into nothing more than a pleasant memory. Along with the others, she yelled "Good-bye!" and "See you next summer!" but her thoughts were elsewhere.

And then she was on the top step of the bus, able to see the faces of the mob awaiting the returning campers. She searched the blur of faces, finally spotting a big, husky, curly-haired man in a short-sleeved shirt, his tie slightly askew.

"Dad! Dad!" She waved frantically, caught his eye, and was happy to see his arm waving back with equal enthusiasm. But where were the others?

Hoisting her knapsack and gripping her suitcase, she pushed herself through a sea of hugs and suitcases until she herself was enveloped in a massive bear hug.

"Hiya, pumpkin! Have a good time?"

Crushed against his chest, Phoebe managed a muffled "Yeah." Finally he released her from his grip and held her at arm's length. "Look at you, all brown and rosy-cheeked. You're going to make the rest of us look positively sickly."

Phoebe looked around. "Where *are* the rest of us?"

But her father didn't hear her. He was looking at his watch and frowning. "The bus was late, and I've got to get back to the paper. C'mon, pumpkin." He lifted Phoebe's suitcase, and she followed him to the station wagon.

"Where is everyone?" she asked again as she climbed into the car.

Her father tossed the suitcase in the back, got in, and started the car. "Well, let's see. One of you is at the junior high getting registered, another's at a protest rally or something like that, and the third's out spending money. Does that account for everyone?"

With very little effort, Phoebe was able to figure out which sister was where. But that still left one missing person.

"Where's Mom?"

Her father was concentrating on the road. "She's at a department meeting at the high school."

Phoebe was confused. "What department?"

"That's right—you haven't heard the big news. Your mother's been offered a job at the high school, teaching English. She just got the call last week."

"You mean she's going to substitute like she did last year?"

"No, no—she's going to be a real full-time teacher. How about that?"

Phoebe thought about it. "What does she want to do that for?"

"Well, you kids are all old enough to take care of yourselves. And your mother wants a new challenge. I think it's a great idea."

A new challenge. A great idea. Phoebe wasn't so sure. She'd never liked it much when her mother substituted. She liked coming home and finding her mother there, fixing her a snack. Now she'd have to fix her own.

"It'll be rough for a while," her father mused, frowning the way he did when he was actually talking to himself. "She'll be under a lot of pressure. . . . Maybe we can get a cleaning person once a week. . . ."

"Hey, Dad," Phoebe interjected, "I got a medal for archery."

"Huh? Hey, that's great, pumpkin." Then he frowned again. "I suppose we could use the money."

Phoebe turned to him in alarm. "There's no money, Dad. It's just a medal."

But her father didn't seem to be listening. "Of course, teachers' salaries aren't that great, but even so, with four kids, and college tuitions being what they are . . ."

A thought occurred to Phoebe. "Hey, Dad, if we need money, I could get a job."

Her father took one hand off the wheel and ruffled her hair. "I think we can manage without that. For the time being, at least."

But the idea still intrigued Phoebe. "Maybe I could start babysitting. Lydia makes a lot of money babysitting."

"Babysitting?" Her father shook his head. "You're hardly more than a baby yourself."

Phoebe pondered this. A baby? One minute she was old enough to take care of herself; the next, she was a baby. This was getting a little confusing.

And then they passed the big highway sign that declared Cedar Park—A Great Place to Call Home. Phoebe started to bounce up and down.

"Yay, Cedar Park!" Then she looked at her father in surprise. He always yelled that with her when they passed the sign.

But this time he hadn't even noticed. He was looking at his watch. "I'm going to have to drop you off and get right back to the office. Your mother should be home shortly. You'll be okay by yourself, pumpkin, won't you?"

Phoebe's heart sank. "You mean nobody's home?"

"Oh, they'll all be back soon for dinner," her father assured her.

So far, nothing was going quite as she'd anticipated. But there was something else that might work out. "Are we having fried chicken?" Phoebe asked hopefully.

"Well, I'm in charge of picking up dinner. And if you want fried chicken, fried chicken it is."

"Oh. Okay." Fast-food chicken. It wasn't Mom's—but Phoebe guessed it would do.

The car pulled up in front of a big white two-story house shaded by huge oaks. "Here we are," her father announced.

Phoebe had envisioned herself jumping out of the car and running up to the house. But the house was empty, so what was the point? She followed her father up the walk, but was surprised when he headed for the front door. She was used to going in by the side.

"How come we're going in the front?"

"Got a surprise for you," her father replied.

She knew it—they were really all at home waiting for her, and maybe her friends were there, too. Phoebe prepared herself for the cry of "Surprise!" as she followed her father inside.

There was no chorus of "Surprise!" but Phoebe gasped anyway once she was in the living room. For a minute, she thought they were in the wrong house.

"What happened?" she cried.

Her father beamed. "Your mother redecorated. How do you like it?"

Phoebe looked around the room in bewilderment. Everything was white and glass and shiny metal. It looked like one of those fake living rooms she'd seen in a department store—the kind nobody really lived in.

"I guess it's okay," she said finally, grabbing her suitcase and knapsack. "I'm going to take these up to my room."

She was a little nervous as she approached the bedroom she shared with Daphne, but breathed an enormous sigh of relief when she entered. The pale pink curtains still fluttered at the windows, and the flowered spreads still covered the beds.

Daphne's ballet poster continued to reign over her side of the room, and next to the poster were the framed pressed flowers her sister had made. A small bookcase in the corner contained neatly shelved books in alphabetical order.

An identical bookcase stood in Phoebe's corner, too. But hers was nicked and scratched and covered with rings from glasses of milk she'd left sitting too long. She had a poster, too, but it wasn't like Daphne's. Hers showed a bunch of different cartoon animals reading books. Ms. Wrenn at the public library had given it to her a long time ago.

And while Daphne's bed was neatly made, with only a pillow sham perfectly centered on it, Phoebe's was covered with old stuffed animals and rag dolls that were missing portions of their bodies.

Phoebe pushed some of them aside and tossed her

suitcase and knapsack on the bed. She was about to open the suitcase when she heard her father call.

"Here's your mother now. I'll see you later, pumpkin!"

Phoebe ran downstairs and looked out the picture window. Her mother was getting out of a car, but she wasn't alone. Two unfamiliar women were with her.

Phoebe wanted to run out to her, but the presence of two strangers held her back. Instead, she waited for her to come in.

As her mother approached the house, Phoebe studied her. She looked different. Her brown hair now had blonde streaks in it, and it was pulled away from her face. And she wasn't wearing her usual jeans. She had on a light-blue suit Phoebe had never seen before.

But when she came inside and saw Phoebe, her face lit up with a familiar smile and she opened her arms wide. "Hello, darling! I'm so glad you're home. Did you have an absolutely wonderful time at camp?"

Phoebe hugged her, but she was aware of the two ladies watching.

"Camp was super. We put on this play and I was in it."

"How wonderful! You'll have to tell me all about it later." She turned to the two ladies. "This is my baby, and look at her! All grown up!" She introduced the strangers—Dr. Something and Mrs. Something Else. "They're my colleagues, Fee. Isn't it wonderful! I'm a real teacher now!"

The women laughed, and one of them said something like "You don't know what you're getting into!" as she sat down. Phoebe tried to perch on the arm of the new sofa, but it wasn't soft and comfortable like the old one and she gave up after losing her balance twice. Her mother had left the room and the two women started talking about textbooks and lesson plans and other stuff Phoebe didn't think was very interesting.

She wandered into the kitchen where her mother was making coffee.

"Isn't this exciting, Fee? Your mother's got a career!"

Phoebe scratched an old mosquito bite. "Great."

Her mother looked at her quizzically for a moment, then set the coffeepot down to put an arm around Phoebe. "Guess what we're having for dinner tonight?"

Phoebe shrugged. "Dad says he's picking up chicken."

"*After* the chicken."

Phoebe looked up at her. "Double chocolate fudge cake?"

Her mother planted a kiss on her forehead. "In honor of your homecoming. Now, why don't you go unpack while I talk with my new colleagues? And then you can tell me all about your camp experiences."

Phoebe gave her mother a quick hug and then skipped upstairs. Okay, maybe her homecoming hadn't quite lived up to her expectations. But the double chocolate fudge cake was a good omen. Everything would soon get back to normal.

She unpacked quickly, piling up most of the clothes to shove into the laundry basket. Then she removed a small packet of tissue tied loosely with a string. Carefully, she peeled back the layers of paper until she uncovered four shiny pins. She examined each one to make sure they looked just as perfect as they had when she'd

13

finished making them in arts and crafts. The white enamel was so clean and bright it made the yellow letter *D* look almost like real gold.

The pins were for the Doodlebugs—her and Linn and Melanie and Jessica. They'd called themselves that since the first grade, when they'd become best friends. Phoebe couldn't even remember where the name had come from. It wasn't like a real club, with meetings and all that, but they still called themselves the Doodlebugs, and sometimes they'd use the silly words they'd made up long ago for their secret Doodlebug language.

Now they had official Doodlebug pins. Phoebe placed them carefully on her bookcase and went out to the hall to the little alcove where a telephone sat next to a chair. She didn't have to look up the numbers—she knew them by heart.

She dialed Jessica's number first, hanging up when she heard a busy signal. Then she dialed Melanie's. It was busy, too. The two were probably talking to each other, Phoebe decided, and dialed Linn.

A familiar voice answered the phone.

"Doodle-doo! It's me! I'm back!"

"Fee! Oh, I'm so glad you're home! I've got so much to tell you!"

"Me, too! Can you come over?"

"Hold on—I'll go ask."

A few seconds later, she was back. "My mom says she'll bring me over after dinner. I'll call Melanie and Jessica, okay?"

"Great! I can't wait to see you guys. You won't believe some of the stuff that went on at camp!"

"Well, *I've* got a surprise for *you!*"

Another surprise? Phoebe'd had just about as many as she could handle in one day. "What is it?"

Linn giggled. "You're not going to believe it! I'll see you around seven." Then she hung up, without even saying "buggle-buggle," the official Doodlebug good-bye.

Phoebe replaced the receiver, wondering what Linn's surprise could be. A new pen pal? Doodlebug T-shirts?

It didn't really matter. The gang would get together and have a great time, just like always. So what if her homecoming hadn't been what she'd expected? So what if her mother had a job and the living room was different? Some things—like best friends—never changed.

3

PHOEBE CONTEMPLATED the now-empty living room. The schoolteachers had left, her mother was upstairs changing clothes, and Phoebe now had a moment to examine the brand-new room. She looked around. It was clean, it was tidy, and it definitely looked brighter than the old room had. But she didn't like it. It was too neat, too clean, and it didn't feel like home.

Her thoughts were interrupted by the knob turning on the front door. She watched curiously as the door opened slowly and a fair head peered in furtively.

"Cassie! Hi!"

"Shhh!" Phoebe's pretty sister whispered, her arms full of bags. "Fee, quick—help me get these upstairs before Mom sees them."

What a terrific greeting, Phoebe thought. But she

obliged, grabbing a bag and peeking inside. All she could see were layers of tissue paper. "What's in here?"

"C'mon," Cassie said urgently. She tossed her head in a futile attempt to get her long blonde hair out of her wide-set blue eyes. "Where is Mom, anyway?"

"She's right here."

Mrs. Gray entered the room, and Phoebe was glad to see her mother looking much more normal in jeans and one of her father's old shirts.

Her mother eyed the bags with suspicion. "Cassie, what have you got there?"

Cassie bit her lower lip and forced an uneasy smile. "Just some clothes. You said I could get some new stuff for school."

"I didn't say you could buy out the store." She took the bag Phoebe was holding and began rummaging through it, as if she was looking for something.

"Everything was on sale," Cassie offered nervously.

Mrs. Gray pulled out a receipt and looked at it. Her mouth fell open and she glared at Cassie, who was studying the carpet with unusual concentration.

"Cassie, what is the meaning of this? I said you could buy a sweater. And that was it—*a* sweater."

"But I couldn't make up my mind between these two sweaters," Cassie said plaintively. "And then I needed a skirt to go with them. And Mom, I absolutely had to get some shoes."

Phoebe watched her mother. She was getting what they all called "the look"—tight lips, narrowed eyes, head cocked to one side. Unfortunately, Cassie didn't notice.

"You don't want me to go to school in rags, do you?" she continued. "Besides, I figured now that you're teaching full-time, maybe I could get some new clothes. . . ."

"I did not get a job teaching full-time so you could go out and charge an entire new wardrobe! Good grief, Cassandra, did you really think you were going to get away with this? You're going right back to the mall tomorrow to return every single item in these bags."

"But, Mom . . ." Cassie wailed.

Phoebe left the room. Watching Cassie and her mother go at it was like watching a rerun of a TV show she'd seen a zillion times.

"But I can't wear last year's shoes, Mom. Nobody's wearing flats with straps anymore!" Phoebe heard her sister whining as she climbed the stairs.

She went into her bedroom and threw herself down on the bed. Who cared about whether or not shoes had straps, anyway? *She* certainly didn't. Shoes were what covered your feet, that was all, and if it didn't get so cold in the winter, she'd be perfectly happy to go without them. What happened to people when they got to be teenagers? she wondered. Well, at least whatever it was didn't happen to everyone. Lydia didn't seem to care much about shoes and clothes. Phoebe decided she would be like Lydia.

She got up and wandered to the window, brightening when she saw a thin, dark-haired figure walking slowly toward the house. Even from a distance, Phoebe could see one hand on her nose, pushing back the glasses that were constantly slipping.

"Daphne!" Phoebe yelled out the window. But as

usual, her next-oldest sister didn't hear her. She was probably off in one of her daydreams.

Phoebe ran out of the room, nearly colliding with a disconsolate Cassie.

"She won't even let me keep the shoes," Cassie muttered. Phoebe tried to look appropriately sympathetic, but kept going.

"Hey, Fee, I forgot—how was camp?" Cassie called out after her.

"It was okay! I got a medal for archery."

Cassie nodded vaguely, turned, and dragged her bags toward her room.

Well, at least Cassie remembered she'd been away, Phoebe thought. That was probably about all she could hope for from *her*. But she knew for sure Daphne would want to hear all about camp.

When Phoebe got downstairs, Daphne was already in the kitchen sitting at the table. Her large, usually dreamy eyes were focused anxiously on their mother as Mrs. Gray examined an official-looking paper. But she jumped up when Phoebe entered, throwing her arms around her.

"I'm so glad you're home! How was camp?"

"It was super! We put on this play—" Phoebe began, but their mother interrupted.

"Daphne, what's *PHED*?"

"Physical Education," Daphne explained, wrinkling her nose. "It's required."

"And can I assume *CONAMLIT* means Contemporary American Literature?"

Daphne nodded happily. Her normally placid face

was glowing. "I got to choose some of my classes," she told Phoebe. "Junior high is so different from elementary school. They don't treat you like a baby."

"I don't feel like a baby," Phoebe objected, but Daphne was now addressing their mother.

"It's *huge!* I feel like I could get lost in that school."

"But you'll have two sisters watching out for you," Mrs. Gray reminded her. "Won't that be nice? Three of you in the same school."

Suddenly Phoebe felt funny again. Of course she'd known that this year Lydia, Cassie, and Daphne would be in junior high and that she'd be the only one still in elementary school. But she hadn't really thought about it.

They'd all be together—and she'd be alone. But not really alone, Phoebe assured herself. There were her friends, and they'd all be starting school together just like always.

"C'mon, Fee, tell me more about camp," Daphne urged.

Phoebe collected her thoughts. "We had a great arts and crafts counselor. I made you something you can wear on your first day at junior high."

"Oh, Fee, that's so sweet! I can't wait to see it."

"Come on upstairs and I'll show you," Phoebe said. They started out of the kitchen, but just then the phone rang. Phoebe was the closest to it. "Hello?" she answered. Then she handed the phone to Daphne. She didn't have to say who it was. When the phone was for Daphne, it was always Annie, her one and only best friend.

"I'll take it upstairs," Daphne said, running out of the room.

20

Phoebe waited until she heard Daphne say, "Hi! Did you get history for second period?" Then she hung up the phone and sat back down. She might as well wait till dinner to give out the gifts. Maybe by then she'd be able to get some attention.

"Mom, I made you something, too," Phoebe said.

"Really? How nice!" her mother replied. But she was distracted by the sound of a car honking outside. "Oh, no—here's your father now, and I haven't even made a salad. Fee, wash this lettuce, will you?" She wiped her hands on a towel and went out the kitchen door.

Fee rose slowly, went to the sink, and turned on the water. As she rinsed the lettuce, she began to feel more than a little sorry for herself. Her first day home from camp, and what was she doing? Washing lettuce, all alone in the kitchen. What kind of homecoming celebration was this, anyway?

But she wasn't alone for long. Within a few seconds, the kitchen was in its usual state of commotion. Her father came in and placed a huge bucket of chicken on the table, and her mother began pulling dishes and glasses from the cupboard. Daphne returned to set the table, while Cassie joined Phoebe at the sink to cut up vegetables. Mr. Gray greeted each one with a "Hiya, pumpkin!" For a moment Phoebe wondered if he always called them that because he couldn't keep their names straight.

"Who'd you get for English?" Cassie asked Daphne.

"Ms. McBain."

"Oooh, ick!" was Cassie's response. "You'll have to write tons of papers."

"I like writing papers," Daphne replied mildly.

21

"Well, whatever you do, don't sign up for volleyball in phys ed," Cassie advised. "It's brutal."

"I played volleyball at camp," Phoebe interjected. "I liked it."

Cassie grimaced. "Too sweaty." She turned to Daphne. "Try to get archery. You barely have to move."

Phoebe tried again. "I got a medal in archery. And I learned how to do a swan dive, too. The coach said I'm turning into a pretty good swimmer."

This comment actually seemed to interest Cassie. At least she looked thoughtful. Then she whirled around to their father.

"Dad, could we have a swimming pool built out back? There's plenty of room, and then we wouldn't have to go to that crummy community center pool. And Phoebe could practice her swan dives," she added kindly.

Mr. Gray looked up from the newspaper, appearing to seriously consider Cassie's request. He smiled briefly. "No."

Cassie sighed and returned to tossing the salad.

"Okay, everyone," Mrs. Gray announced, "let's eat."

They all gathered at the table. Phoebe was just about to pass the bucket of chicken when her mother said, "Wait a minute—somebody's missing."

A look of exaggerated dismay crossed Mr. Gray's face. "You mean there's another one?"

"Oh, Daddy," the others groaned. It was his standard joke whenever one of them wasn't there.

Daphne's forehead wrinkled. "Did Lydia go to that rally in Chicago?" she asked worriedly.

"Maybe it turned into a riot," Phoebe offered.

Her mother frowned at her. "Don't talk nonsense," she said, but now she looked worried, too.

As if on cue, the kitchen door swung open, and a lean, gangly girl with short tousled hair ambled in. Her cheeks were flushed with excitement.

"Sorry I'm late," Lydia said breezily. "Hey, Fee— welcome home!"

Phoebe eyed her oldest sister with undisguised admiration. "How was the rally?"

"Fantastic," Lydia pronounced, sitting down and reaching for the chicken bucket at the same time.

"What's this week's cause?" Mrs. Gray asked.

"Nuclear disarmament."

"Big deal," Cassie murmured.

Lydia turned to her with flashing eyes. "It *is* a big deal, you dork."

"No name calling at the dinner table, please," Mrs. Gray said automatically.

"This is only the most vital issue of the decade!" Lydia exclaimed. "Dad, I really think you should do an editorial on nuclear disarmament."

Mr. Gray clapped a hand to his head in dismay. "Gee, why didn't I think of that!"

"This is not a laughing matter!" Lydia's voice was rising.

"Pumpkin, I was doing editorials on nuclear disarmament before you could even pronounce it."

"Oh." Lydia was only momentarily deflated. "Well, you should do more. If all nations don't learn to resolve their problems and stop producing weapons—"

"Cassie," Mrs. Gray said suddenly, "what are you doing?"

"I'm taking the skin off my chicken. I'm on a diet."

Daphne pushed her glasses up her nose and peered at her. "You don't need to be on a diet, Cassie. You look fine just the way you are."

Lydia focused a stern eye on Cassie. "Half the world is starving and you're throwing away food," she intoned dramatically. "Besides, how can you talk about dieting when I'm discussing possible world devastation?"

Phoebe didn't want to hear about either. And her expression must have indicated so because her mother suddenly said, "Why don't we hold off on nuclear disarmament and diets for a while and let Fee tell us about camp?"

At last! Phoebe put down her fork and began. "Well, I got to ride horses a lot. And I learned to jump over a fence. I was a little scared at first, but once I got the hang of it, it was great."

"If we don't have nuclear disarmament," Lydia muttered darkly, "there won't be any horses to ride. Or people to ride them."

Phoebe pretended not to hear her. "And I did lots of arts and crafts. I even made presents for everyone. Can I go get them now?"

When her mother nodded, she ran out of the room and upstairs to gather the gifts. At least this would hold their attention for a while.

She raced back to the kitchen with her arms full. "Mom, this is for you. I pressed the flowers myself, and I made the frame."

"Fee, this is beautiful! I know just where I'll hang it."

"And this is for you, Dad." Her father took the object and examined it carefully.

"Hey, this is, uh, great. What is it?"

"It's a free-form clay sculpture. My counselor said it's very creative."

Her father nodded. "And it will make an excellent paperweight. Thank you, pumpkin."

"Here, Cassie." She handed her sister a length of green material. "It's a scarf. I silk-screened it."

Cassie's eyes lit up. "Oooh, this will go perfectly with that green blouse I bought." Then the corners of her mouth turned downward. "That is, if I don't have to return it."

Mrs. Gray sighed wearily. "We'll see."

Cassie beamed. "Thanks, Fee!"

Phoebe briefly wondered if Cassie was thanking her for the scarf or for giving her an excuse to keep the blouse. But then she distributed the rest of the gifts—a carved leather belt for Lydia, a beaded necklace for Daphne—and basked in their exclamations of delight and thanks. She began speaking rapidly, hoping to hold their attention. "I was in a play, too. We did *Guys and Dolls*. I was one of the guys."

"Hey, I saw that movie on TV," Lydia said, sniffing. "I thought it was sexist."

Mrs. Gray looked pensive. "As I recall, it *does* present some outmoded views of women as sex objects."

"Hey, I remember that play," Mr. Gray said. "I thought it was very clever."

Lydia scowled. "Dad, you're such a chauvinist."

"Lydia, how can you say that?" Mrs. Gray exclaimed. "Your father's always supported women's rights."

Mr. Gray acknowledged the fact with a little bow. "Besides," he said, grinning slyly, "if I were a chauvinist, do you think for one minute I could survive being surrounded by females like this?"

"Personally," Cassie said loftily, "I think all this feminist stuff is silly. I like being a girl."

This set Lydia off and running. "That's got nothing to do with feminism," she yelled, and then it seemed like everyone was talking at once.

Phoebe glanced over at Daphne, who was sitting quietly. Her face had a glazed-over expression that Phoebe knew meant she was off in her own private dreamworld.

Phoebe had the sudden feeling that if she were to disappear that very moment, nobody would even notice. She put down the chicken leg she'd been gnawing. It didn't have much taste.

"Hey, Mom, can I get dessert?"

"What? Oh, sure, Fee. What I mean, Cassie, is that a woman can be feminine and still take charge of her own life."

Silently, Phoebe went to the refrigerator to get the dessert. Here she'd been gone for two whole months and all they wanted to talk about was feminism and nuclear disarmament. Even the double chocolate fudge cake she carried to the table didn't do much to lift her spirits.

At least Daphne had come back to earth. "Fee, I love this necklace. It's very artistic! I wish they had jewelry-making classes at school."

"Oh, it's easy," Phoebe started to say, but the word *school* had caught their father's attention.

"Speaking of school, let's see your fall schedule," he said to Daphne, and in the next few seconds, the conversation shifted to Daphne's first year in junior high.

Phoebe just sat there, silently chewing her cake. Then she remembered something.

"Mom," she said, not caring if she interrupted Cassie's lengthy instructions to Daphne on what to wear to junior high, "Jessica and Melanie and Linn are coming over after dinner. Is that okay?"

Phoebe knew it would be. But just announcing it had made her feel a little better. Her best friends would be interested in her camp stories. They wouldn't ignore her or talk about feminism. She could count on them.

With these cheering thoughts, she blocked out the table conversation and turned her full attention to the one other thing she could count on—the double chocolate fudge cake.

4

WHEN THE DOORBELL RANG an hour later, Phoebe leaped off her bed and ran downstairs. "I'll get it!" she shrieked as she raced across the living room.

Her mother looked up from her book. "You don't have to scream," she remarked mildly, but Phoebe didn't pay any attention. She was getting her voice in shape for what was to come.

Sure enough, the moment the door opened, Linn's squeals and Phoebe's cry of "Doodle-doo" could have broken the sound barrier—or at least a few eardrums. When Phoebe and Linn finally managed to break their embrace, Mrs. Gray's eyes were still closed in pain. She opened them long enough to offer a weak, "Hello, Linn—good to see you."

Linn immediately calmed down. "Oh, hello, Mrs.

Gray," she said in a very adult voice. She looked around. "I just *love* your new living room."

Mrs. Gray smiled slightly. "Why, thank you, Linn." She rose from the sofa, clutching the textbook she'd been reading. "I'll let you girls have the room to yourselves," she murmured, beating a hasty retreat.

Linn immediately pulled away from Phoebe and struck a pose.

"Well? What do you think?"

"About what?"

Linn made a face. "C'mon, Fee! You haven't even looked at me!"

Phoebe looked. There wasn't any big difference as far as she could see. The same round, pink-cheeked face, the same dimples, the same light-brown hair—no, wait . . . maybe the hair *was* a little different.

"You cut your hair?"

"Yeah, yeah, but that's not it. Fee, look at my T-shirt!"

Phoebe was mystified. It was just a plain blue T-shirt, nothing special.

Linn couldn't wait. "I'm wearing a bra!"

"Oh. . . ."

Linn tossed back her shoulders and stuck out her chest. Now that she knew what to look for, Phoebe could just make out the lines that showed faintly through the shirt.

"Well? How do I look?"

"Fine," Phoebe said uncertainly. What was the big deal? Lots of girls wore bras. Personally, Phoebe hoped she'd be like Lydia, who didn't really need one and hardly ever wore one. She'd always thought it would feel like a harness. "How does it feel?" she asked.

"Sort of funny. I only got it last week. I've been wearing it every day so I can get used to it. I even wear it to bed sometimes." Linn walked to the mirror hanging over the fireplace and examined her profile. "I think I'm getting a real figure. What do you think?"

"Yeah, I guess so," Phoebe replied. "Is that the big surprise you were telling me about?"

Linn gazed at herself in the mirror, lowering her eyelids and smiling dreamily. "There's something else, too. Something you can't see."

"What?"

With dignity, Linn turned to face her and spoke in hushed tones. "I'm a woman now."

At first Phoebe didn't know what her friend was talking about. Then she remembered the pamphlet her mother had given Daphne called *You're a Woman Now*. Her mouth fell open. "You got your period?"

Linn nodded.

"But Daphne doesn't even have hers yet!"

"Girls develop at different ages," Linn said, as if she was reciting from the pamphlet. "I just happen to be an early developer."

She almost sounded like she was proud of it! Phoebe stared at her in dismay. She hoped *she* wouldn't be an early developer. Cassie moaned and groaned every month when she got hers. And Lydia said it was a real mess.

Linn misread her expression. "Don't worry, Fee. You'll get yours." She grinned. "Mel and Jess are practically dying of jealousy, too."

"You're kidding!"

Linn looked slightly offended. "No, I'm not kidding. C'mon, Fee, you know you're jealous. You just don't want to admit it. Now tell me what went on at camp."

Still feeling a little dazed by all of Linn's new developments, Phoebe joined her friend on the couch and began recounting her camp stories. At least Linn was still the same old Linn when it came to listening. She was the perfect audience, nodding, laughing, looking shocked, and saying "Oh, wow!" at all the right times.

"Were there any cute boys there?" she asked when Phoebe paused to take a breath.

"There were no boys, period. It's an all-girl camp."

"Oh. Too bad."

Phoebe looked at her quizzically and was about to ask "Who'd want boys around, anyway?" when the ringing of the doorbell prevented her from pursuing the question.

This time she barely cracked the door open before another round of squeals began.

Tiny Melanie was bouncing up and down, her blonde curls bobbing. "Fee, you look exactly the same!"

Phoebe giggled and rolled her eyes. "Well, of course I do—I've only been gone two months! What did you expect?"

Jessica wasn't a squealer. In fact, her voice hardly ever rose above a whisper. She hugged Fee, and then stepped back.

"What do you think of my hair?" she asked anxiously.

"What's different about it?"

Jessica's face fell. "Can't you tell? I had a perm. It's just for body, really. Don't you think it looks fuller?"

"I guess so," Phoebe said doubtfully.

"I've got something new, too," Melanie said excitedly. "Guess what it is."

Phoebe squinted. "You're not wearing a bra, too, are you?"

Melanie shook her head sadly. "No, my mother says I'm not ready yet. But look!" She pulled wisps of blonde curls behind one ear.

Phoebe's mouth fell open. "You're wearing earrings!"

Melanie nodded proudly. "I had my ears pierced. Aren't they great?"

Phoebe examined the small gold balls. "Did it hurt?"

"Not too much. Now I'm going to get earrings to match all my clothes."

Phoebe shook her head in amazement. "Gee, I go away for two months and you guys go crazy."

"I'm getting mine pierced next week," Linn announced. "I might even get two holes in each ear."

"Me, too," Jessica chimed in. "I just hope I don't faint when I see the needle."

"It's not a needle," Melanie assured her. "It's more like a gun."

Jessica went a little pale.

"Let's all get our ears pierced together," Linn suggested. "Maybe we could all get the same earrings, too! And we could wear them on the first day of school."

Phoebe shuddered. "No, thanks." The mere thought of someone sticking anything through her ears gave her the creeps.

"Oh, c'mon . . ." Linn began.

Luckily, Melanie interrupted. "Linn, did you tell Phoebe the big news?"

"I know, she got her period and she's wearing a bra," Phoebe said.

"No, this is something else, bigger than a bra," Jessica offered.

Melanie let out a whoop. "*Anything* would be bigger than Linn's bra."

The three laughed hysterically.

Phoebe smiled uncertainly. "Okay, what's this big news?"

Linn curled herself up on the sofa, hugged her knees, and lowered her eyelids demurely. "I have a boyfriend."

Phoebe gasped. "What?"

"And he's sooo cute," Jessica said. "I swear, he was the cutest guy at the pool this summer. Cuter than the lifeguard, even."

"Nobody's cuter than that lifeguard," Melanie objected. "Not even Chip."

"Chip?" Phoebe could barely say the name she was in such a state of shock.

"That's his name," Linn murmured, an odd, glazed expression appearing on her face. "Oh, Fee, he's so wonderful. I'm in love."

Phoebe looked at her in wonderment. "You mean you've been going out on dates and stuff like that?"

Linn's face fell for a second. "No, not exactly. My parents won't let me. But I saw him at the pool practically every day. And yesterday I met him at the mall and he bought me an ice cream."

"I don't get it," Phoebe said. "If you can't go out on dates, how can he be your boyfriend?"

"He just is," Linn replied vaguely. "I think he wants to kiss me."

"Linn!" Melanie and Jessica shrieked in unison.

Phoebe couldn't believe what she was hearing. "You're not going to let him, are you?"

"Why not?"

Phoebe wasn't sure. "Well, you could get germs or something. You can get diseases from kissing."

Linn rolled her eyes. "Oh, honestly, Fee."

"Besides," Phoebe continued, with more conviction, "I'll bet you don't even know how to kiss a boy. It's not the same as kissing your father, you know."

"I know that," Linn replied haughtily. "But I can learn, can't I? I mean, there's got to be a first time for everything."

Jessica spoke up softly. "You can practice, like I do."

Melanie looked at her curiously. "How do you practice?"

Jessica blushed. "I use this old teddy bear. . . ."

But before she could even finish, Linn and Melanie became hysterical again.

Phoebe didn't join in. She slumped down on the sofa. "I think kissing boys is gross."

"Oh, Fee," Jessica sighed, "you wouldn't say that if you saw all the cute boys at the pool this summer."

"Yeah, you haven't seen Larry Sims yet," Melanie added.

Phoebe stuck her finger in her mouth and made a gagging noise. "Larry Sims? Debbie Sims's brother? He's a creep. Remember how he used to chase us on the playground?"

"He's changed," Linn informed her. "He got his braces off, and honestly, he's positively gorgeous."

"Roger Feinstein just got braces," Jessica said thoughtfully. "But you know, I don't think they look so bad. They sort of make him look older."

Phoebe listened to all this in bewilderment. What was going on here? She groaned loudly. "I can't believe school's going to start in three weeks." Now maybe they could all talk about that.

"I can't wait for school to start," Melanie said, bouncing on the sofa. "This year I'm definitely going to find a boyfriend."

"Fee, wait till you see what I got to wear on the first day," Linn said excitedly. "It's almost exactly like the outfit on this month's cover of *Seventeen*. Do you know what you're going to wear?"

Phoebe shrugged. "Just my jeans and a T-shirt, I guess."

"But Fee," Jessica said worriedly, "we're in the sixth grade now. We don't want to look like fifth graders."

"I'm trying to get my mom to buy me some of those new flats," Linn remarked. "You know, the kind without straps."

She sounded just like Cassie. Phoebe felt sick.

"I hope we get in the same class," Melanie said. "I want Miss Lacey. She's so cool."

Now they were getting into safe territory. Phoebe breathed a sigh of relief. "Me, too. Lydia had Miss Lacey three years ago, and she loved her. But Daphne had Mrs. Kowalski, and she liked her a lot."

Linn made a face. "She's fat."

"So what?" Phoebe asked.

"I definitely want Miss Lacey," Melanie said. "She's got great clothes."

"Yeah," Linn agreed. "I like the way she looks.

35

Especially when she wears her hair down and it curls around her shoulders. I wish my hair would do that."

Were these really the Doodlebugs talking like this? With this thought, Phoebe suddenly remembered something. She jumped up. "Wait till you guys see what I made us at camp!" She ran upstairs, grabbed the packet of pins, and raced back down again.

Slowly, dramatically, she unwrapped the packet and handed each of them a pin.

"Oooh, how pretty," Jessica crooned.

"Yeah, they're really neat," Melanie said. "What's the *D* for?"

"*Doodlebug*, stupid!" Phoebe replied.

"Gee, thanks, Fee," Linn said. "I'm putting mine on right now."

Jessica looked a little worried as she pinned hers on. "But if we wear these to school, everyone will want to know what the *D* stands for."

"We'll just tell them it's a secret!" Phoebe said.

Now Melanie was frowning. "But that sounds so babyish."

"Maybe not," Linn said, looking thoughtful. "You know, now that we've got these pins, maybe we ought to make the Doodlebugs into a real club."

Phoebe looked at her with interest. "What do you mean?"

Linn fingered the pin. "My mother has this old pin sort of like this in her jewelry box. She told me that when she was in high school they had these social clubs, and they wore pins and had secret passwords and all kinds of stuff like that."

"What were the clubs for?" Jessica asked.

"Oh, mostly just to have parties and dances. The boys had clubs too, and sometimes they'd have a party together with a girls' club. And if a boy and a girl really liked each other, they'd give each other their pins to wear."

Melanie's eyes were sparkling. "Oooh, that's neat! You could give your pin to Chip!"

"Hey, wait a minute," Phoebe objected. She hadn't slaved over making those pins just so Linn could give it away to some dumb boy.

Linn giggled. "I wonder what Chip would say if I told him about the Doodlebugs."

Now Phoebe was really shocked. "You're not going to tell him, are you?"

Melanie grabbed a pillow from the sofa and held it close to her face. "Oh, Chip, darling," she crooned in a deep voice. "Buggle-buggle, doodle-doo, I love you, my darling!" And then she covered the pillow with loud kisses.

Phoebe watched glumly as Linn and Jessica doubled over giggling. "I got a letter from my pen pal in Australia while I was at camp," she said. But no one seemed to hear her.

Linn sat up suddenly. "Hey, Jess, did you bring the stuff?"

"What stuff?" Phoebe asked as Jessica began rummaging in her bulky purse. Triumphantly, her friend pulled out a large plastic pouch. Melanie squealed with delight.

"It's makeup," Jessica told Phoebe. "My mother's old stuff. She said I could have it."

"What for?"

"We're going to try it out," Melanie said excitedly. "All the girls wear makeup in junior high."

"But that's a whole year away," Phoebe objected.

"We need a year to practice," Linn explained, taking the bag from Jessica and poking through the assorted bottles and tubes.

Cassie wandered into the room. "Hi, kids," she said. "What are you up to?"

Linn looked up eagerly. "Oh, Cassie, can you help us? Jessica's mother gave us some old makeup and we want to try it."

A flicker of interest crossed Cassie's face. "Let me see," she said, taking the pouch from Linn. She nodded approvingly as she examined the contents. "Hey, there's some good stuff here. Yeah, sure, I'll help you."

Jessica, Melanie, and Linn chattered happily as Cassie led them upstairs. Reluctantly, Phoebe followed. Playing with Jessica's mother's makeup wasn't quite what she'd had in mind for the evening. "You sure you wouldn't rather play Monopoly?" she suggested hopefully. Nobody seemed to hear her.

Cassie paused in the hallway and frowned. "I wish I had my own room."

Phoebe knew what she meant. Lydia wouldn't appreciate an army of girls putting on makeup in the bedroom she shared with Cassie. And Daphne was reading in their room. "We could use the bathroom," she suggested halfheartedly.

"Good idea," Cassie said, leading her entourage into the bathroom.

Their house was old and the bathroom unusually

large. Even so, it was crowded with the five of them. Phoebe perched on the edge of the tub while the others clustered around a large mirror set above a dressing table. Cassie took charge.

"We'll begin with eyeshadow," she announced in a voice that rang with authority. "You should apply it with a light touch, extending the color just slightly beyond the lid."

The girls hung onto her every word. "I want to try the green," Linn said.

"Pass me the purple," Jessica requested.

Cassie gave her a brief but withering look. "That's *mauve*, dummy."

Jessica wasn't offended. "Mauve," she repeated, as if memorizing it for future reference.

Phoebe watched the girls slop the goop on their faces. "I got a letter from my Australian pen pal," she tried again. "It's winter there right now."

Linn's lips barely moved as she stood still so Cassie could apply pink powder to her cheeks. "I wonder if I could get a male pen pal—from England, maybe? Wouldn't that be neat—a guy with an accent!"

Phoebe sniffed. "You wouldn't be able to hear his accent in a letter."

"But I could imagine it," Linn replied.

"Shut up," Cassie ordered her. "I'm using a lip liner on you. Do you want your lips thinner or fuller? Fuller is sexier."

Oh, who cares? Phoebe thought. She was beginning to feel more and more irritable.

Cassie stepped back from Linn and studied her work.

"It's a definite improvement," she announced decisively.

Linn admired her reflection. "Gee, Cass, thanks."

Melanie and Jessica looked suitably impressed. "Wow, Linn," Melanie said. "You look at least fifteen."

Yeah, Phoebe thought, like a fifteen-year-old clown.

"Do me next!" Jessica begged. Cassie started on Jessica, while Melanie added another layer of color to eyelids that already looked like miniature rainbows.

"C'mon, Fee—try some," Linn urged. "It's fun!"

Resignedly, Phoebe joined them at the mirror, picking up a lipstick.

"What's going on in here?" Lydia stood at the door. "Don't you guys have anything better to do?"

Phoebe looked at her gratefully. At least Lydia realized how idiotic this all was. Her oldest sister looked pointedly at the lipstick Phoebe was clutching and shook her head sadly. "Don't you realize that makeup is just another device to make women submissive?" Still shaking her head, she turned and left the doorway.

Phoebe wanted to run after her and explain that this wasn't her idea, but she was distracted when Linn started brushing her cheeks with blusher. "Quit that," Phoebe said sharply, pushing her friend's hand away.

Linn stared at her. "What's the matter with you?"

"Nothing," Phoebe muttered. She went back to her place on the edge of the bathtub.

"Now, look at Jessica," Cassie said triumphantly. The others squealed. Phoebe didn't even bother to look.

Something was wrong here. Everyone was giggling and laughing and acting silly, and they weren't even noticing that Phoebe wasn't joining in. Here she was, in her own home, in her own bathroom, with her own best friends, and she felt like she wasn't supposed to be there.

Funny, just a few hours ago she was sitting on a bus, all excited about getting home and being with her friends. And now she was here.

But this wasn't the way it was supposed to be. Something was definitely wrong.

5

THE MORNING SUNSHINE poured into the bedroom, beckoning Phoebe outside. But she made no effort to move. She just sat there and watched Daphne at the mirror, brushing her hair.

"C'mon, Daphne, let's go," Cassie called from across the hall.

Daphne tugged at a lock of hair that stubbornly refused to lie flat. "I'm coming!"

"Where are you guys going?"

"Cassie wants to take me to the mall. She says I have to look at the new fall fashions to get some ideas about what to wear to school."

Phoebe's forehead puckered. Daphne had never cared much about clothes. Mostly, she dressed like Phoebe did—jeans and T-shirts—though hers were always clean and neat.

"How come you can't wear what you always wear?"

"Cassie says kids dress up more in junior high. She says it's okay to wear jeans, but not all the time. And she says they have to be a special kind of jeans." She shook her head and sighed. "I guess I should pay more attention to what I wear now that I'm starting junior high."

"Why?"

Daphne gave her hair one last tug. "I don't know. Cassie says that's just the way it is." She paused at the doorway. "Want to come with us?"

Phoebe shook her head. Poor Daphne, she thought. Well, at least *she* had another year before anyone started bugging her about clothes. She thought briefly about Linn and the others, already talking about what they were going to wear to school. But Linn was always getting excited about one thing or another and then forgetting about it. Phoebe remembered a time two years before when Linn swore she wouldn't go anywhere without her kitten. Eventually she got tired of lugging it around. Maybe she'd get sick of clothes and makeup, too.

She got up and wandered across the hall. Lydia was at the open door of her closet on her hands and knees, surrounded by piles of papers, magazines, and a few odds and ends of clothing.

"What are you doing?"

There was a muffled groan, and Lydia backed out from the closet. "Mom says I've got to get this closet cleaned out. You wouldn't believe the stuff I'm finding. Look at this." She pointed to an old shoe box.

Phoebe peered inside. "Paper dolls? How come I didn't get them?" Paper dolls, like just about everything else in the family, got handed down from sister to sister.

Lydia stood up and brushed some dust from her knees. "I guess they got lost in the closet. They must be at least five years old. I haven't played with paper dolls since I was, oh, I guess eight or nine." She glanced into the box and poked around. "Seems a shame to throw them away. They're really in good condition. But I guess you're too old for these now, too."

Phoebe looked a little wistfully at the pile of cut-out figures and colorful paper dresses. "Yeah, I guess so. Is that the phone? I'll get it."

She ran out to the alcove in the hallway. "Hello?"

"Fee? Hi—it's me."

"Hi. Did you ever get all that makeup off?"

Linn giggled. "My father had a fit. He said if he ever caught me with that stuff on my face again I'd be grounded for life."

I don't blame him, Phoebe thought.

"Listen," Linn continued, "you wanna go to the pool? It's supposed to get really hot this afternoon."

Phoebe paused. Last night, being with her friends hadn't been much fun. On the other hand, she didn't want to hang around the house all day.

"C'mon," Linn urged. "Maybe Chip will be there. Don't you want to see him?"

Well . . . maybe she was a tiny bit curious.

"Okay," she said finally. "I'll meet you there in about half an hour."

Twenty minutes later, with a T-shirt and shorts over a bathing suit, Phoebe got into the front seat of the car next to her mother.

"Mom," she said, as her mother pulled out of the driveway and headed toward the community center, "when you saw Linn and the others last night, did they seem . . . *different* to you?"

"Not really," her mother replied. "But I only saw them for a few seconds. Why?"

"They're acting really weird."

Her mother sighed. "Fee, you're going to have to be more specific."

Phoebe shifted around uncomfortably. "Well, they keep talking about dumb stuff. Like boys and clothes and junk like that."

She was annoyed to hear her mother laugh. "They *are* starting a bit early, aren't they? But I suppose it's inevitable. You're all growing up so fast these days."

"*I'm* not interested in boys and clothes and that kind of stuff," Phoebe replied indignantly.

Her mother was still smiling. "Don't worry—you will be."

Phoebe slumped back in her seat. Her mother didn't understand at all.

"It's only natural, Fee," she continued. "When you grow up, you find new interests, and . . ."

Phoebe stopped listening. Her mother kept talking, but Phoebe just stared out the window.

"I won't be home this afternoon," she heard her

45

mother say as they pulled up in front of the community center. "Do you have a way to get home?"

"Sure," Phoebe replied, anxious to get out of the car. "I'll be home by five."

She ran around to the back of the center and went through the gate leading to the pool. A bunch of kids were in the pool splashing and yelling, but she didn't see Linn and the others in the water.

"Fee! Over here!"

Phoebe discovered the source of the voice lying on a towel by the side of the pool. Melanie and Jessica were identically positioned.

"How come you're not in the water?" she asked, flopping down next to Linn.

She didn't move. "I'm working on my tan."

"I don't want to get my hair wet," Jessica explained. "It'll get frizzy."

Phoebe looked around for evidence of the famous boyfriend. "Where's Chip?"

"He's not here yet," Linn replied. "Oh, Fee, just wait till you see him. He's sooo cute."

"I know, I know, you told me." Phoebe pulled off her shorts and T-shirt, casting a longing look at the water.

"But I still don't think he's as cute as the lifeguard," Melanie stated firmly. "Did you see him, Fee?"

Phoebe looked in the direction her friend indicated. A muscular, blond-haired boy—no, *man*—was sitting in the high lifeguard's stand. A couple of teenage girls in bikinis had his full attention.

"Isn't he wonderful?" Jessica sighed.

"Mmmm," Melanie murmured. "I wonder how I can get him to notice me."

Phoebe was shocked. "Mel, he's *old!* He must be in high school!"

Melanie giggled. "So what? I still like to look at him."

"Hey, guys," Linn said suddenly, "I just had the most incredible idea." She sat up, her eyes gleaming. "I've got my birthday coming up next month. I'm going to ask my mother if I can have my party at night—with boys!"

Jessica's eyes widened and Melanie clapped her hands.

Phoebe's mouth fell open. "Why?"

"You could make it a dance," Melanie said excitedly.

Jessica looked worried. "But I don't know how to dance. Do you?"

"We'll learn," Linn assured her. "Hey, Fee, do you think maybe we can get Cassie to teach us?"

Phoebe didn't reply. The memory of Linn's last birthday party flashed through her mind. She'd invited all the girls from the fifth grade, and her mother had hired a magician who pulled a real bird out of a handkerchief. *That* had been a great party.

Phoebe stood up. "Wanna see my swan dive?" And without waiting for a response, she headed off to the diving board.

Birthday parties with boys and dancing. She didn't know how to dance and she didn't want to learn. She was so dismayed she could barely remember the proper form for her dive.

But she hit the water cleanly, and if the dive wasn't perfect, it was probably good enough to impress her friends. She swam to the edge of the pool where they were gathered and hoisted herself up. "How was that?"

But they weren't even looking. They had their heads together and were giggling hysterically.

"What are you talking about?"

Melanie leaned forward and hastily whispered something in her ear.

"What?"

But Melanie had leaped up and gone to the edge of the pool, where she jumped in and swam to the center. Phoebe glanced at Jessica and Linn, who were laughing so hard they were shaking. Puzzled, she looked back at Melanie, who was splashing around in the water, dropping underwater and then bobbing back up.

And then Phoebe clapped her hand over her mouth. Melanie's arms were flailing about and she was yelling something. It wasn't a loud yell, but Phoebe caught the word her mouth was forming—*Help!*

Without even glancing at Jessica or Linn, Phoebe leaped up and made a running dive into the pool. She swam vigorously to her floundering friend, grasped her firmly under the arms (thank goodness she'd learned drown proofing at camp!), and dragged her to the side of the pool.

As soon as they reached the edge, Melanie pulled herself free of Phoebe's clutches. With one hand on the rim, she coughed violently. Phoebe looked for the lifeguard. He was so busy looking at the bikini-clad girls he hadn't even noticed the near-drowning!

"Are you okay?" Phoebe asked anxiously. Linn and Jessica had come to the side of the pool and were crouched above them.

Finished with her coughing fit, Melanie turned watery red-rimmed eyes on Phoebe. "What did you do *that* for?" she hissed.

Phoebe looked at her in bewilderment. "To keep you from drowning!"

Melanie's eyes were baleful. "Didn't you hear what I told you?"

Above her, Phoebe could hear Jessica giggling like a maniac. She turned to her blankly, and then stared at Melanie. "What are you talking about?" she asked wildly.

"I wasn't drowning, you idiot!" Melanie groaned. "I was just pretending to drown! To get the lifeguard's attention!"

Phoebe's mouth fell open. She turned to Jessica and Linn, who by now were clutching each other and laughing so hard there were tears streaming down their faces.

Melanie rolled her eyes, shook her head sadly, and pulled herself out of the water. "Dummy," she muttered.

Slowly, Phoebe hoisted herself up and sat on the edge of the pool. "Look," she heard Jessica say comfortingly to Melanie, "the lifeguard didn't even see you. You can try it again tomorrow."

"As long as Fee doesn't try to save me," Melanie grumbled.

At that, Phoebe jumped up and glared at Melanie coldly. "You won't have to worry about *that*. You can just go ahead and really drown for all I care."

"Oh, come on, Fee . . ." Linn began.

But Phoebe wouldn't let her finish. A burning anger filled her. "I can't believe you'd do such a stupid thing!" she yelled at Melanie.

Jessica gasped. "Fee! The lifeguard will hear you!"

Melanie tossed her head. "You just don't know anything about flirting, Fee. You're so immature."

Linn hastily intervened. "It's not her fault, Mel. She just didn't hear you."

But Phoebe didn't want Linn's defense. "It doesn't matter whether I heard her or not. I think what you did was really stupid."

Jessica looked thoughtful. "I thought it was kind of neat."

"Neat!" Phoebe couldn't believe what she was hearing. "It wasn't neat! It was—it was the dumbest thing I've ever seen!"

Melanie stamped her foot and glared at Phoebe. "Oh, grow up!"

Phoebe glared back at her. Without saying a word, she pulled on her shorts and T-shirt and gathered up her towel. "I'm going home."

"Now, wait a minute," Linn said placatingly, "you don't want to go now. You haven't even seen Chip yet!"

"I can live without seeing Chip," Phoebe snapped.

"But my mother's coming for us at four," Linn argued.

"I can get home on my own." And without even saying good-bye, Phoebe marched to the gate.

She headed toward the pay phone to call her mother. But then she remembered that her mother wasn't home. It would be a long walk home—but her anger alone would probably give her enough energy.

How could her best friends act like such jerks, she wondered furiously as she walked. Pretending to drown to get a lifeguard's attention—how idiotic could a person get? What had gotten into them?

Her pace slowed as the heat of the midafternoon caused the sweat to pour down her. The hotter she got, the angrier she felt. How could three people change so much in two months? Her mother said it was natural, that it was all part of growing up. And Melanie had told her to grow up. Well, if that was what growing up was all about, Phoebe had one response. No, thanks.

6

P HOEBE!"

Phoebe looked up from the book she wasn't really reading. Her mother was standing in the doorway, irritation clearly written all over her face.

"This is the third day in a row you've been lying around your room moping."

"I'm not moping," Phoebe replied defensively. "I'm reading."

"You're moping," her mother said decisively. "And it's an absolutely gorgeous day outside. Now, I want you to get up and do something."

"There's nothing to do."

"What are your friends doing?"

Probably looking for swimming pools to drown in,

Phoebe thought. But all she said was, "Nothing I'd want to do."

Her mother was beginning to look impatient. "Well, think of something *you* want to do."

"Like what?"

"Good grief, Fee, you're not a baby anymore! I'm not going to plan your activities—you're old enough to amuse yourself." Then she sighed wearily and sat down at the foot of Phoebe's bed. "Is something bothering you?"

"No." That wasn't exactly true—but her mother wouldn't understand if Phoebe tried to explain, so what was the use?

Mrs. Gray rose. "Then get out of this room and find something to do." With a look that clearly said "and I mean it," she left.

Reluctantly, Phoebe pulled herself off the bed and went to the window. The brilliant sun and cloudless sky did little to lift her spirits.

She wandered downstairs to the kitchen, where Daphne and her best friend Annie were looking at a little magazine and talking.

"There's a drama club," Annie was saying. "That might be fun."

Daphne's eyes widened. "You mean, *act*? On a stage? In front of an audience?"

Annie shook her head vehemently. "Oh, no! I mean behind-the-scenes work. You know, painting scenery, that sort of stuff."

"What are you guys talking about?"

"Junior high," Daphne said. "This book tells about

all the clubs they have. We're trying to decide what to sign up for."

"Oh." Phoebe lost interest. Junior high was just another thing not to look forward to.

She went back up to her room, got the book she'd been looking at earlier, and decided to take it outside. *That* should make her mother happy.

A few minutes later, she settled herself on the front steps with a glass of lemonade and opened her book. But the glare from the sun made it hard to read, and after a few minutes she gave up and closed the book.

There were three more weeks till school started. Funny—just a few short days ago she'd been looking forward to these three weeks. Now they loomed in front of her like empty hours with nothing to fill them.

And what would she do when school started? Would the other girls be acting like Linn and Melanie and Jessica, giggling about boys and clothes and makeup? Is that what she had to look forward to? Phoebe couldn't remember ever having felt so miserable in her life. It was as if a big, dark cloud was floating above her, following her around.

A car pulled up in front of the house and her father got out, carrying a tennis racket. He waved to the driver, then joined Phoebe on the stoop.

"Whatcha reading, pumpkin?"

Phoebe held up the book so her father could see the cover.

"*Charlotte's Web*," her father read. "Didn't I read that to you kids when you were little?"

"So what?" Phoebe said testily. "Can't I read it now?"

Mr. Gray stepped back and held up a hand as if to ward off a blow. "Okay, okay—don't bite my head off."

She hadn't really meant to sound quite so irritated. "Sorry, Dad," she said.

Her father shook his head in resignation. "Kids," he murmured, ruffling her hair and then strolling into the house.

That big, dark cloud was now firmly planted on her head. Behind her, the door opened. Daphne stuck her head out.

"Fee, Mom's calling you. She's upstairs."

Phoebe dragged herself off the stoop and went inside. Her mother was standing in the hallway outside the bathroom and she looked angry.

"What is the meaning of this?" She pointed to the bathroom floor, where Phoebe had left her pajamas that morning.

"Oh. I guess I forgot to put them in the laundry basket."

"Phoebe, you have got to start picking up after yourself! You're not a baby anymore!"

"Okay, okay," Phoebe muttered, picking up the clothes. When she looked at her mother again, Mrs. Gray was shaking her head.

"Fee, honey, you've got to realize that I'm going back to work full-time. And I wouldn't be doing that if I didn't think you kids were old enough to cooperate and help out. You've got to start acting your age."

"Want me to start wearing makeup, too?" Phoebe asked sullenly.

Her mother's eyes narrowed. "Don't take that tone with me, young lady."

"I'm not a young lady," Phoebe muttered. "I'm just a kid."

Mrs. Gray threw up her hands and walked out.

Phoebe tossed the clothes into the laundry basket and then drifted back to Lydia's room. Lydia was now surrounded by the entire contents of her closet, and was gazing dismally at the chaos on the floor.

"Are you still cleaning out that closet? You were doing that three days ago."

"I didn't know I had a deadline," Lydia said shortly.

Phoebe sat down on the edge of Lydia's bed. "I'm bored," she announced. "There's nothing to do."

"You can help me pick up this junk," Lydia offered.

"No, thanks," Phoebe replied. She watched Lydia pick up an ancient-looking pair of tennis shoes with two fingers and carry them gingerly to the wastebasket.

"I'm *boooored!*" she said again.

"Quit whining."

"I can't help it," Phoebe whined. "There's nothing to *dooo*." She dragged the last word out as long as possible.

"Oh, Fee, you're such a baby."

Phoebe glared at her. "I am *not* a baby."

"Then grow up!"

Phoebe flinched. With as much dignity as she could muster, she stood up and walked out of the room. She went across the hall to her own room and threw herself down on her bed, feeling sort of like crying. But no matter how hard she scrunched her face, the tears wouldn't come.

"Fee! Get the phone, will ya?"

I can't, Phoebe thought—babies can't answer the telephone. But she got up and went out into the hall. After all, she didn't have anything else to do.

"We're going to the mall to look at the new clothes." Linn's voice on the other end of the line was disgustingly cheerful. "Wanna come?"

"No, thanks."

"Melanie's not mad anymore."

Phoebe wasn't surprised. Melanie got over being mad as quickly as she got mad. But that didn't change Phoebe's mind. "I still don't want to go to the mall."

"Why not?"

"I don't want to look at clothes. I'm not interested in clothes."

"How can you not be interested in clothes?" Linn sounded incredulous.

"Because I'm not! That's—that's teenage stuff."

"So what? We're almost teenagers. C'mon, Fee—"

"I don't want to go to the mall!" Phoebe yelled.

Linn was silent for a moment. "Gee, Fee, what's your problem? You've been acting really weird lately."

Look who's talking, Phoebe thought. But she bit her lip. She really didn't want to get into a discussion about it. "I can't go to the mall because I'm doing something else."

"Yeah? What are you doing?"

Phoebe thought rapidly. "I'm going to the library."

"The library!" She might as well have said "the moon" from the way Linn responded. "Why are you going to the library?"

"Because I feel like it!"

"Oh. Well, if you see a new Betsy Drake book, will you check it out for me?"

Phoebe groaned to herself. She should have guessed Linn would be getting into Betsy Drake. But all she said was, "Yeah, sure. I gotta go."

After she hung up the phone, it occurred to her that the library wasn't a bad idea. At least it was air-conditioned.

She passed Lydia on the way out. Phoebe would have preferred to walk by without speaking, but was forced to ask a question. "Where's Mom?"

"She's in the study working on lesson plans. Better not bother her."

"I have no intention of bothering her," Phoebe said coldly. "Just tell her I went to the library."

Lydia didn't even seem to notice her tone. "Okay."

The library was only a twenty-minute walk from her house. Phoebe ambled along slowly in the steamy afternoon heat, remembering how she used to go to the library every week. She felt like she hadn't been there in ages.

As she approached the imposing, gray stone building, a wave of comfortable familiarity passed over her. Memories of story hours and afternoons spent curled up in a beanbag chair with a favorite book quickened her pace as she climbed the stairs to the entrance.

When she went inside, there was her favorite librarian, Ms. Wrenn, holding court in the children's room. The pretty, redheaded woman looked a bit harried as she directed a cluster of little kids to the storytelling pit at the far end of the room. But she spotted Phoebe and greeted her warmly.

"Good to see you, Phoebe! Can I help you find something?"

Phoebe returned the smile. "I'm just going to look around, if that's okay."

"Of course it's okay! I wish I could chat with you, but I've got a story hour now," Ms. Wrenn replied. She motioned toward a book cart laden with shiny covers as she turned to rejoin the story group. "A new Betsy Drake book just came in. If you grab it, you could be the first on your block!"

Phoebe nodded politely, but she didn't move over to the cart. She'd never much liked Betsy Drake books. Everyone else was crazy about them. Cassie'd read each one about a dozen times. All the girls in her bunk at camp were reading them. Phoebe had tried one but found it boring—it was a "real life" sort of book, with girls talking about bras and getting their periods. She should probably pick up the book for Linn—but then Linn already seemed to know enough about bras and periods.

Phoebe wandered over to the shelves, scanning the rows until she found an old favorite—*Mary Poppins Opens the Door*. She took it to one of the beanbag chairs not far from the story pit and snuggled up.

Every now and then she glanced over at the story group, where the rapt faces of the children were glued to the picture book Ms. Wrenn was holding up. The librarian wasn't having an easy time of it, though. First she had to stop to tell a bunch of teenagers by the paperback rack to keep the noise down. Then a girl who looked a little younger than Phoebe interrupted her to ask for help. Ms. Wrenn told her to wait until the story was finished.

Phoebe watched the girl approach the shelves and stare at them blankly. The poor kid looked totally helpless.

"Can I help you find something?" Phoebe asked her kindly, trying to sound like Ms. Wrenn.

The girl brightened. "I'm just looking for something good to read."

Phoebe rose from her chair. "What kind of books do you like?"

The girl pondered this. "I like stories with make-believe people."

Phoebe studied her. She looked about eight or nine. Phoebe thought back to her own favorite books at that age.

"Wait here," she instructed the girl, going over to the card catalog. Then she returned to the shelves, examined a row, and pulled out a book. "How about this?"

"*The Borrowers*," the girl read from the cover. "What's it about?"

"It's great," Phoebe assured her. "All about these little tiny people who live under a clock in a house."

"Okay," the girl said, starting to take the book to the circulation desk. Then she paused and looked back over her shoulder at Phoebe. "Hey—thanks."

"You're welcome." Feeling pleased with herself, Phoebe went back to her chair. No sooner had she sat down then a couple of little boys approached her.

"Hey, you know where the dinosaur books are?"

"Sure." Phoebe got up again and led them to a bookcase. The boys didn't bother to thank her, but she didn't care. She gazed around the room to see if there were any others who looked like they needed help.

A short while later the story hour was breaking up and Ms. Wrenn came over to her. "I saw you helping those kids," the librarian said. "That was very nice of you."

Phoebe grinned. "It was fun!"

Ms. Wrenn looked around the room and sighed. "It gets so busy in here sometimes, and there's no way I can run a story hour and help other kids at the same time. I had some volunteers from the junior high this summer, but they've all gone and quit on me." She smiled lightly. "I guess they didn't want to spend the last few weeks of vacation in a library."

Phoebe looked around. She couldn't think of a better place to spend the last few weeks of vacation. It was quiet and peaceful—and there was no one to bug or nag her. The children's room—a place where no one would tell her to grow up!

"I could be a volunteer!" she told Ms. Wrenn.

Ms. Wrenn looked at her doubtfully. "I don't know, Phoebe. You're a little younger than our usual volunteers."

But Phoebe was already getting excited. "I know a lot about the library. I know how the card catalog works and everything. And I could even help with story hours. I'm a good reader—listen!" She grabbed a picture book from the top of a shelf and began reading it out loud, with lots of expression. When she finished a page, she looked up at Ms. Wrenn eagerly.

The librarian looked thoughtful. "Maybe I could use you, Phoebe. If it's all right with your parents. . . . Of course, you know I can't pay you."

"Oh, that's okay," Phoebe said quickly, thinking that her parents would probably pay the library just to get her out of the house.

Ms. Wrenn smiled and nodded. "Have your mother call me."

Phoebe practically skipped out of the building. No more lying around her room feeling bored. No more listening to sisters and friends telling her to grow up. She could hide out in the library, safe from the real world with nothing to do but read fairy tales to little kids and share her favorite books. And nobody could call her a baby for it. After all, you didn't hear people yelling at Ms. Wrenn to grow up!

7

PHOEBE LEANED AGAINST the circulation desk and surveyed her little world. This was only her third day at the library, but already she felt like she'd found a place where she belonged.

It hadn't been difficult convincing her mother to let her work there. Just as she'd suspected, her mother was happy to see her occupied.

She'd gotten mixed reactions from everyone. The Doodlebugs thought she was nuts, giving up the last few weeks of summer to work in a library. Lydia, on the other hand, was actually enthusiastic. "I always thought working in a library might be fun."

Daphne approved, too—and even expressed some admiration. "You're really brave, Fee. I could never go up to total strangers and ask them if they need help."

"They're mostly little kids," Phoebe reminded her. But Daphne's shyness didn't discriminate for age.

Cassie was less impressed. "Who ever heard of spending the summer in a library? Nothing ever happens in a library. It's always the same."

That was exactly what Phoebe liked about it. The library today was exactly the way it was yesterday, and just the way it had been when she herself had come regularly for story hours. Sure there were new books, and different posters on the walls—but it was still the same place. It *smelled* the same. A library was a place you could count on, Phoebe thought. Peace and quiet. No surprises.

This morning, for example, she had busied herself the same way she had yesterday and the day before: shelving books and generally straightening up after the preschool story time. Okay, maybe that *was* kind of boring, but she could count on being interrupted every now and then by kids needing help. One boy told her he was going to Canada with his parents on a holiday, and Phoebe showed him where he could find books about Canada. Then she helped a mother find picture books for her little girl. The best interruption was when the girl who had taken *The Borrowers* returned—and was thrilled to find out there were more books about the little people.

There were routines and regular jobs that made Phoebe's day comfortable and familiar, but there were also the odd little questions and the different people— Ms. Wrenn called them patrons—needing help. They made the day interesting.

"You're a big help, Fee," Ms. Wrenn told her several times. Each time Phoebe basked in the praise. Every day she helped gather the books for the story times, and when there weren't a lot of patrons needing help, she sat in on the story hours, acting as Ms. Wrenn's assistant. She'd sit on the edge of the group, watching for any kids who might start horsing around, punching their neighbors, or looking like they had to go to the bathroom. But usually she could let herself get swept away into the story, just like the little ones, and that was the best. Her friends could have their boyfriends and clothes and makeup—she had the library.

Phoebe picked up a stray book from a table, examined the call number on its spine, and returned it to its proper place. Then she glanced at the clock. It was a quarter of two—almost time for the afternoon story hour.

She hurried to the workroom in back of the circulation desk, where she found Ms. Wrenn on the floor unpacking some new books.

"Five more copies of the new Betsy Drake," the librarian announced. "Think that'll be enough?"

Phoebe rolled her eyes. At least ten girls had come in during the past three days asking for it. She smiled knowingly. "Well, you know how those preteen girls feel about Betsy Drake."

Ms. Wrenn's upper lip twitched a bit, but then she noticed the clock on the wall. "Heavens, it's story time and I don't even have the books ready." She jumped up and went to her desk.

"I'll get them," Phoebe offered.

Ms. Wrenn gratefully handed her the list. "Thanks, Fee. I'll get the projector set up for the movie."

Phoebe went back out to the shelves and set about collecting the books. It was always hard trying to do this quickly—she was distracted by titles she remembered. This one about the wild things, for example. She had a vivid memory of Lydia reading it to her and Daphne when she was four and Lydia was seven. Daphne had been scared by the weird-looking creatures and cried. Phoebe, on the other hand, had loved them, as had Lydia. Those were the good old days, she thought wistfully.

For a brief moment, she contemplated bringing the book home to show Lydia. Would she remember it? Maybe . . . but then she'd probably tell Phoebe to grow up and stop reading baby books. With a small sigh of regret, she replaced the book on the shelf.

Quickly, she gathered the rest of the books and brought them to the story pit where Ms. Wrenn was winding the film.

"You know, Ms. Wrenn," Phoebe said thoughtfully, "I think maybe I'll be a librarian someday. It's so nice and peaceful here, and nobody hassles you."

Ms. Wrenn laughed lightly. "Don't count on that, Fee."

Phoebe wanted to ask her what she meant, but the kids were starting to come in for story time. A handful of five- and six-year-olds ran into the pit. These were the regulars, and they confidently planted themselves on the cushions, their faces expectant. But there was usually a new kid or two who hung back with an expression of uncertainty. Phoebe always looked out for those, leading them by hand into the pit and showing them where to sit. Then she'd step back and survey the group with a professional eye, making sure they were evenly spaced and could all see the screen.

"Good afternoon, boys and girls, and welcome to story time," Ms. Wrenn said, with a big smile. "Today, our story time is all about the creatures who live in the sea. We're going to hear a story about an octopus and a story about a sea horse. But first we're going to see a movie about two little goldfish."

"I have a goldfish!" one little boy yelled.

"Me, too," another piped up.

"I have *two* goldfish!"

"I have *three!*"

"How nice," Ms. Wrenn said quickly, putting a finger to her lips. "But we can't get started until we're all quiet, okay? And if anyone has a problem while we're watching the movie or listening to the stories, just raise your hand and my assistant will help you."

The kids turned and looked at Phoebe, who smiled at them kindly. Then Ms. Wrenn started the film, and they all focused their attention on the screen.

Phoebe tried to watch the film, but the words *my assistant* kept floating through her head. They made her feel official and important. Special.

When the film was over, Ms. Wrenn let the kids stand up and stretch, then she led them in a few finger-play games. Afterward they settled back on their cushions and the stories began. While Ms. Wrenn read, Phoebe glanced around the room to see if anyone needed help.

A large, heavyset woman had just come in and was standing in the center of the library. She had a book in her hand and was tapping her foot impatiently, as if she was in a store and couldn't find a clerk to wait on her.

As unobtrusively as possible, Phoebe got up and left the pit. Walking toward the woman, she had a feeling she'd seen her before. It was the hair that looked familiar—all puffed up and stiff, sort of an orangy-red color.

"Can I help you?" Phoebe asked politely.

The woman gave her a thin, brief smile. "I'd like to see the librarian. Immediately."

Phoebe looked back at the pit. Ms. Wrenn was in the process of holding up a book so the kids could see the picture inside.

"She's busy right now. If you're looking for a book, maybe I can help you."

This time the woman didn't bother to smile at all. "I don't need your help, little girl. I want to talk to the librarian."

Phoebe resisted an urge to snap back, "Don't call me 'little girl.' " Instead, she strained to keep her voice calm and even.

"Well, she's right in the middle of a story time. . . ."

The woman made a gesture as if to brush Phoebe aside and strode briskly toward the pit. Phoebe ran alongside her.

"Are you sure I can't help you?"

The woman ignored her. "Ms. Wrenn," she called out loudly.

The librarian was just closing the picture book. She looked up. "Yes?"

"I must speak with you. *At once*." She made it sound like an order.

Ms. Wrenn seemed momentarily taken aback by the woman's strident tone. The smile she managed looked a little forced.

"The story time will be finished in about five minutes. If you'll have a seat, or perhaps browse a bit . . ."

"I have no time to browse," the woman stated firmly. "I must talk to you now. I assure you, it's a matter of grave importance."

Ms. Wrenn looked like she was about to say something, then thought better of it. She threw a quick, helpless look at Phoebe.

"Phoebe, would you mind taking over and reading this book?"

Phoebe took the book from her and sat down in her place at the front of the pit. The kids were starting to get restless, and as she tried to quiet them, she kept glancing curiously at the woman confronting Ms. Wrenn. What could possibly be so important that it was worth interrupting a story time?

"My daughter brought this book home, and I happened to take a look at it. I tell you, Ms. Wrenn, I was shocked—no, *appalled*—to think you would have such trash in the library."

Phoebe strained to hear the librarian's response, but Ms. Wrenn had taken the woman's arm and was firmly directing her toward the workroom behind the circulation desk.

"C'mon, read the story!" Phoebe heard a kid demand. She turned her attention to the book. But even as she concentrated on reading the story with expression, she couldn't help wondering what was going on. What was this trash the lady was talking about?

The questions faded as she got caught up in the story. It was pretty good, actually—all about a sea horse in search of a rider. She remembered what Ms. Wrenn had told her about the importance of establishing eye contact, so after every other line, she glanced up at her audience. She was amazed to see the kids gazing at her just the way they looked at Ms. Wrenn when the librarian was reading. It gave her tingles.

"And they lived happily together on the bottom of the sea, forever and ever." She closed the book. The kids sat there, still looking at her. Now what? she thought frantically. She tried to remember what Ms. Wrenn said at the end of story times.

"Now you can look at the books on the table here and pick out the ones you'd like to take home."

The kids jumped up and ran to the table. Some adults, mothers and fathers, drifted in and began collecting their kids.

Phoebe wondered if the angry woman was still back in the workroom with Ms. Wrenn. Did she dare go and see? Why not, she decided—after all, she had to tell the librarian she'd finished. . . .

Phoebe was just about to rap on the workroom door when it flew open. The heavyset lady stood there, her back to Phoebe.

"I'll be more than happy to fill out your complaint forms, Ms. Wrenn."

Phoebe quickly stepped aside as the lady turned and came through the door. Now she could see her face, and she certainly didn't *look* happy. In fact, her face pretty much matched the color of her hair.

"We'll certainly consider your objections seriously, Mrs. Lane," Ms. Wrenn said smoothly, but her forehead was puckered.

The name rang a bell in Phoebe's head. Mrs. Lane— of course! Barbie Lane's mother. Barbie was a friend of Cassie's.

Mrs. Lane inhaled sharply. "They aren't just *my* objections, I assure you. I know a number of parents who would be most disturbed if they realized you were handing out books like these to young, impressionable minds."

Ms. Wrenn started to speak, but Mrs. Lane wasn't finished. "And I'll be very interested to find out what other kinds of trash you have on these shelves."

Ms. Wrenn's voice became less than friendly. "We don't carry trash in this library, Mrs. Lane."

The woman sniffed. She looked like a pig when she did that, Phoebe decided. A pig with an orange mop on its head.

Mrs. Lane turned abruptly and marched out of the library. Phoebe looked apprehensively at Ms. Wrenn, who was staring after her.

"What's going on?"

Ms. Wrenn didn't answer at first. Then she indicated the book she was holding.

Phoebe recognized it. It was the new Betsy Drake book—the same one they'd just received five more of.

"I don't get it. What's she so angry about?"

71

Ms. Wrenn sighed. "Mrs. Lane doesn't think this book is suitable for twelve-year-olds. She thinks it shouldn't be out on the shelf. In fact, she wants to remove all the Betsy Drake books from the library."

"Oh," Phoebe said. Well, it was no great loss as far as she was concerned. She wouldn't miss them. She just hoped Mrs. Lane didn't have any objections to Phoebe's favorite books.

"She didn't say anything about the Marguerite Henry books, did she?"

Ms. Wrenn looked at her blankly. "What?"

"You know, those horse books."

Ms. Wrenn shook her head. "No, I don't think those books would bother her."

"Well, that's a relief," Phoebe said happily.

Ms. Wrenn nodded slowly, but didn't really look like she was listening.

"Well, I guess I'd better get home."

Ms. Wrenn nodded again, and then seemed to actually see Phoebe. "Oh—of course. Thanks for taking over for me, Fee. I'll see you tomorrow."

"Absolutely," Phoebe said. "Bye."

Ms. Wrenn smiled at her. But her eyes looked funny, like she didn't really feel like smiling. Like something was bothering her.

"I think we should all be more concerned with pollution," Lydia said as she passed the salad bowl. "You wouldn't believe the disgusting stuff they spray these vegetables with."

Mr. Gray eyed the lettuce suspiciously. Mrs. Gray sighed.

"Please, Lydia, not at the dinner table."

"Anything exciting happen at the library today?" Cassie rolled her eyes as she said this, making it clear she didn't think anything exciting could ever happen at the library.

"As a matter of fact," Phoebe said smugly, "I got to read to the kids in a story hour."

Cassie didn't look very impressed, but Daphne said, "That's neat," and Mrs. Gray looked interested.

"Ms. Wrenn must think a lot of you, Fee, to let you run a story hour. That's a lot of responsibility."

"Well, I didn't exactly run it. This lady was making a big fuss about having to talk to her right away, so Ms. Wrenn let me read the last book." She turned to Cassie. "It was Mrs. Lane, Barbie's mother. Boy, was she angry. She wouldn't even let Ms. Wrenn finish the story hour."

Mr. Gray chuckled. "Yes, I can't imagine any story hour standing in the way of Shirley Lane."

"*David,*" Mrs. Gray murmured.

"What was she so angry about?" Cassie asked.

Before Phoebe could reply, her mother spoke. "I think I know what this is all about. Shirley Lane called me this morning. She's upset about some book Kimmie brought home from the library."

"Who's Kimmie?" Phoebe asked.

"That's her younger daughter," Mrs. Gray explained. "I think she's your age, Daphne."

"What's this terrible book she's so worked up about?" Mr. Gray asked.

Phoebe jumped in. "It's the new Betsy Drake book," she said importantly. "I forget the title."

Cassie actually looked interested. "I didn't know there

73

was a new Betsy Drake book. Can you get it for me tomorrow?"

"If it's still there," Phoebe said.

"What do you mean, 'If it's still there'?" her father asked.

"Mrs. Lane said Ms. Wrenn should take it off the shelf and not let any kids check it out."

"Wait a minute!" Lydia said. "She can't do that! That's—what do they call it?"

"Censorship," Mr. Gray said. He turned to Phoebe. "Is that what Mrs. Lane wants?"

Phoebe shrugged. "I don't know. Ms. Wrenn thinks she wants to get rid of all the Betsy Drake books, not just that one."

Cassie looked aghast. "You're kidding! Those are the best books I've ever read!"

Lydia grinned. "Those are the *only* books you've ever read."

Mrs. Gray looked thoughtful. "You know, I've heard a lot about those Betsy Drake books, but I don't think I've ever actually read one. Do you have any of them, Cassie?"

Cassie nodded. "I've got two paperbacks."

"Well, I'd like to borrow them. I want to see what she's making such a fuss about."

Lydia looked at her mother approvingly. "That's the spirit, Mom! Don't let her get away with this!"

Phoebe stared at her. "What's the big deal? They're dumb books."

"They are not," Cassie said vehemently. "You're just too young to appreciate them."

"Do you think they're good books, Lydia?" Mrs. Gray asked.

"They're okay, I guess. I read them when I was Daphne's age." Her tone implied that it had been centuries ago, instead of just two years before.

Mr. Gray was frowning and shaking his head over the brussels sprouts. "Censorship," he said under his breath. "Book banning. What's wrong with these people, anyway?"

"I'm just glad she's not trying to get rid of the books I like," Phoebe said.

Lydia looked at her sternly. "That's a pretty selfish attitude."

Phoebe glared right back. "So what?" It wasn't much of a response, but it was all she could come up with at the moment.

"*Girls,*" Mrs. Gray said automatically. She directed her attention to Phoebe. "What does Ms. Wrenn have to say about all this?"

"She didn't really say much of anything," Phoebe replied. "She gave Mrs. Lane some forms to fill out."

"Complaint forms, probably," her mother said. She turned to her husband. "Remember last year when that church group made such a fuss over *Ms. Magazine* in the library? Didn't you reprint their complaint form in the paper?"

Mr. Gray nodded. "I think they call it a 'reconsideration request,' or something like that. What I do recall is that I wrote a brilliant editorial, which I assumed convinced everyone to lay off the library. Guess I'm not as convincing as I thought I was."

"It was a very nice editorial, dear," Mrs. Gray said, reaching over to pat his hand.

"Of course, that magazine was in the adult part of the library," Mr. Gray said. "Maybe these kids' books—what's the author's name again?"

"Betsy Drake," all four girls said in unison.

"Maybe these Betsy Drake books aren't appropriate for kids."

"I really have to read them," Mrs. Gray said again. "As soon as I get these lesson plans done . . . I wonder if she called a lot of other parents?"

Mr. Gray laughed. "Knowing Shirley Lane, she's probably organizing an army to invade the library and take the books by force."

"*David,*" Mrs. Gray said again.

"Just kidding, just kidding. Look, this whole thing will probably blow over. You know how Shirley Lane gets. Remember when she wanted to impeach the mayor? I don't think we need to get really worried about it."

Phoebe looked at her mother, who had that same funny worried look she'd seen on Ms. Wrenn's face that afternoon. She couldn't figure out why they were so concerned. One book more or less, what was the difference? The library had lots of books. As long as they didn't get rid of the good ones, what was the big deal?

8

THE LIBRARY WAS QUIET when Phoebe arrived the next afternoon. Ms. Wrenn was in her office, talking quietly with another librarian.

Phoebe wandered over to the fiction shelves and poked among the *D*'s. As she expected, most of the Betsy Drake books were out, but a couple of battered titles remained. She took one of them off the shelf and opened it to the middle.

"But Mom," she cried. *"All my friends are wearing bras. I feel like an outcast."* Yech, Phoebe thought. She flipped the pages and stopped to read again.

Was Bobby watching her? Did she dare turn around to find out? What if he saw her? What if he thought she had been watching him? She'd die. She'd absolutely die.

"What are you reading?"

Phoebe hastily closed the book and tried to push it back in its place before Ms. Wrenn could see the title. But the cover was obviously too well known to her. She laughed.

"I thought you didn't like those Betsy Drake books."

"I don't," Phoebe said firmly. "I think they're silly. I just wanted to see what that lady was making such a fuss about."

Ms. Wrenn's smile faded. "Yes, Mrs. Lane does seem determined to keep these books out of kids' hands. I thought once she saw the length of our official complaint forms she'd forget about it. But she filled them out properly and returned them late yesterday afternoon after you left."

"Are you going to get rid of the books?"

Ms. Wrenn shook her head. "No. I had a meeting with our advisory board. They read the book Mrs. Lane was so upset about, and we decided her objections didn't warrant removing them from the shelf."

"Oh."

Ms. Wrenn eyed her quizzically. "Do *you* think we should get rid of these books?"

Phoebe shrugged. "I don't care. I think they're pretty dumb."

"Then you don't have to read them," Ms. Wrenn replied. "But somebody else might want to."

That was true, Phoebe supposed. She looked around the almost deserted children's room. "It's quiet today. Anything particular you want me to do?"

"Not really. Why don't you just find something to read until it's time for the afternoon story hour?"

That was just what Phoebe felt like doing. She was right in the middle of a great dragon story. After getting the book, she curled up in one of the beanbag chairs.

There was a girl in the book who trained dragons for riding. Reading the book in the peace and quiet of the library, Phoebe could envision herself doing the things the girl in the book was doing—slaying monsters, rescuing a knight. She felt herself swept away into this wonderful, magical world—a world where a girl could do something that *mattered*. . . .

"Fee! Hey, Fee!"

The magic shattered as the silence was broken, and Phoebe's head jerked up. Linn and Jessica were headed toward her.

Phoebe put a finger to her lips, the way Ms. Wrenn did when people made noise. "Shhh," she hissed as the girls drew nearer. "This is a library! You're supposed to be quiet!"

"We're going to Burger Monster," Linn said in a slightly lower voice. "Wanna come?"

Phoebe shook her head. "I can't. I'm working."

"You don't look like you're working," Jessica commented.

"I'm just, uh, looking at this book to see if it's good to read to the kids." She gestured vaguely around the room. "And I've got lots of other things I have to do."

"Oh, c'mon, you can take a break," Linn urged. "Chip's at Burger Monster."

"And he's got some friends with him," Jessica added, giggling.

Phoebe made a face. "Boys?"

Linn groaned. "Fee, you've gotta get interested in boys sometime! You can't stay a baby forever!"

Phoebe tried to keep the irritation out of her voice. "Look, I'm very busy and I can't just walk out of here."

"Hello, girls." Ms. Wrenn joined them. "Looking for something?"

"Hi, Ms. Wrenn," Linn said. "We just came by to see if Fee could have lunch with us at Burger Monster."

"I told them I was working," Phoebe interjected hastily.

Ms. Wrenn smiled. "Oh, I think we can spare you for an hour. If you want to take a break with your friends, go right ahead."

Linn and Jessica grinned triumphantly. Phoebe sighed.

"Okay," she muttered. Just as she was rising from her chair, a shrill voice pierced the room.

"Ms. Wrenn! We'd like to see you."

A look of dismay crossed Ms. Wrenn's face. Turning, Phoebe saw Mrs. Lane with another lady and a man standing by the circulation desk.

"Let's go," Linn said, but Phoebe put a restraining hand on her arm.

"Wait a sec. I want to hear this."

They didn't have to get any closer. Mrs. Lane's voice carried across the room.

"We came by to find out what you decided to do about those books."

Ms. Wrenn seemed to be choosing her words carefully. "Our board studied your objections very carefully. We had a meeting about it this morning. And even though you certainly made some very interesting points, we decided the books should remain on the shelf."

Mrs. Lane's elaborate hairdo seemed to quiver.

"You know," Ms. Wrenn continued, "That author has won a number of awards for her books. They're very popular."

The other woman sniffed. "Of course they're popular. Children like a lot of things that aren't good for them. It's our responsibility as adults and parents to protect them from those things that aren't good for them."

"What are they talking about?" Linn asked Phoebe.

"Mrs. Lane thinks the library shouldn't have Betsy Drake books," Phoebe whispered.

"Why?"

"Shhh." Phoebe didn't want to miss any of this.

"Have you read many of her books?" Ms. Wrenn asked.

"I haven't exactly *read* them," the woman admitted. "But I know what they're all about."

Then the man put in his two cents. "Trash," he stated firmly. "The books are trash."

Ms. Wrenn ran her fingers wearily through her hair. "Well, that's your opinion, and you're certainly entitled to it."

"I don't want my daughter reading those books," Mrs. Lane said flatly.

"Fine," Ms. Wrenn replied. "Then just tell your daughter you'd prefer she not read them."

The man raised his eyebrows and glared at Ms. Wrenn. "It's not just *her* daughter we're worried about."

Ms. Wrenn smiled thinly. "Then tell *your* daughter not to read the books."

"I don't have a daughter."

"I don't have all day, Ms. Wrenn," Mrs. Lane announced. "Are you telling me you will not take these disgusting books off the shelf?"

"I'm sorry, Mrs. Lane—" Ms. Wrenn began, but the heavyset woman wouldn't let her continue.

"As you may know, there's a town council meeting next week. I am asking the town council president to place this matter on the agenda."

Ms. Wrenn's mouth dropped open. "Don't you think that's a bit extreme? After all, we're only talking about six books."

Mrs. Lane shook her head smugly. "I think the leaders of this community would be very interested to hear about the kind of books you're making available to young people."

"And there may be more than six books," the other woman interjected. "If you're carrying books like this Betsy Drake junk, there's no telling what other kinds of trash you've got in this place." Her eyes darted around the room suspiciously, as if she was expecting some slimy goo to ooze off the shelves any minute.

Ms. Wrenn looked like she was about to lose her patience. "We do not carry trash. Every book in this department has either been reviewed by a member of our staff or been recommended by a reputable source."

"I'm sure the town council will give you ample opportunity to justify your selection procedures," the man said smoothly. "Good afternoon, Ms. Wrenn."

Phoebe watched the three leave the room, and then looked over at Ms. Wrenn. The librarian's face was almost as red as her hair. Linn and Jessica followed Phoebe to her side.

"Are you okay, Ms. Wrenn?" Phoebe asked anxiously.

Ms. Wrenn managed a wan smile. "Oh, sure, Phoebe. I'm just not crazy about these kinds of confrontations." Her forehead puckered. "I've never had a censorship case in the children's room before."

"Are they really going to take away all the Betsy Drake books?" Linn asked. "I haven't even read them all yet."

"Don't worry," Jessica assured her. "They've got them in paperback at the bookstore."

Linn looked relieved, but Ms. Wrenn shook her head. "That's not the point, girls."

Linn didn't bother to ask her what the point was. "C'mon, guys, we gotta get over to Burger Monster. Sorry about your problem, Ms. Wrenn."

"It's not *my* problem. It's the library's problem, and this is a public library, so that means it's everyone's problem."

Linn looked at her blankly. "Oh. Well, c'mon, Fee."

Phoebe followed them out, glancing back at Ms. Wrenn, who seemed to be lost in thought.

"Where's Melanie?" she asked as they walked down the street toward Burger Monster.

"She's grounded," Linn said. "For a week."

Phoebe wasn't shocked. Melanie was always getting herself grounded for one reason or another.

"What did she do this time?"

Jessica giggled softly while Linn explained.

"She faked drowning again yesterday. This time the lifeguard saw her and he jumped in after her."

"It was so romantic," Jessica sighed.

"After he got her out," Linn continued, "and made sure she wasn't dead or anything like that, he called her mother to come get her. When her mom got there, she was really upset and told Melanie she couldn't go to the pool anymore. So Melanie, like an idiot, told her she was faking the whole thing."

"That was pretty dumb," Phoebe agreed.

"No kidding," Linn said. "One minute her mother was practically crying and the next she was furious."

Jessica shook her head mournfully. "So was the lifeguard. He called us brats."

Phoebe couldn't help grinning. "Serves you right."

They had reached Burger Monster, and Linn paused to examine her reflection in the window. "Is my hair okay?"

"Perfect," Jessica said, pausing to check her own.

Phoebe tapped her foot impatiently. "C'mon, you guys, I'm hungry and I have to get back to the library."

Linn led them in the door, stopping just inside the entrance. "There they are," she said, pointing to a booth in the back.

Phoebe wondered which one was Chip. It couldn't be the one with the red hair and freckles who was in the process of sticking two french fries under his upper lip. Definitely not Linn's type. And the serious-looking one with short hair and glasses didn't seem like the type who wanted a girlfriend. He was more the first-prize-at-the-science-fair type. So it had to be the blond.

"Let's get our food," Linn said, and they went to the counter to place their orders.

"I like the one with the french fries," Jessica whispered

to Phoebe as they picked up their bags and proceeded to the booth. When they got there, Linn got in on one side next to the blond-haired boy, and her expression made it clear that this indeed was the wonderful Chip. Jessica followed.

"Hi, Chip," Linn cooed. "This is my friend, Phoebe."

Chip allowed her a lopsided grin.

"Hi," Phoebe said, squeezing in on the other side next to the boy with glasses. On his other side, the boy with the french fries dangling from his mouth leaned forward, moving his eyebrows up and down.

"I am Count Dracula," he croaked. "I want to bite your neck."

Phoebe smiled politely.

"That's Tommy," Linn said, "and that's Leonard."

Leonard turned to her and nodded. His glasses slid down his nose and he pushed them back up with a finger, just the way Daphne always did.

"We already got our food," Chip said to Linn, "but I figured we should wait till you got here before we started eating."

Linn gave him a look of undying gratitude.

Jessica was staring at Tommy/Dracula. When he finally sucked in his french fries, she started to giggle. He smiled gratefully at her and looked very pleased with himself.

In silence, they all opened their bags, took out their hamburgers, and unwrapped them.

"What's that?" Phoebe asked Leonard, who had unwrapped something other than a hamburger.

"It's a cheese fishburger."

"Gross," Phoebe commented.

Leonard took a bite, chewed, and swallowed.

"That's your opinion," Leonard said calmly. "I don't like hamburgers."

Phoebe scowled. "How can anyone not like hamburgers? It's—it's un-American."

She looked around to see if anyone else agreed. But Linn was carefully pouring precise drops of ketchup on each of Chip's french fries, while Jessica was gazing in awe as Tommy lifted his Coke with his teeth and drank it with no hands.

Leonard was still studying her. "Where do you go to school?"

"Eastside Elementary."

"Well, maybe if you went to Westside like me, you'd know there's a Constitution that guarantees me the freedom to eat what I want."

"What are you talking about?"

"We have freedom of choice in America," Leonard said. "I can eat a cheese fishburger if I want to." As evidence, he took a big bite and chewed it with obvious pleasure. "Mmmm." And he punctuated it with a grin.

Phoebe couldn't help grinning back.

"I know all about the Constitution, *and* the Bill of Rights, *and* the amendments. And I know all about freedom of speech and freedom of the press. But I don't remember reading anything about freedom to eat fishburgers."

Leonard wiped his mouth with his napkin. "That comes under the pursuit of happiness."

———

"Don't you think he's cute?" Linn asked her as they walked back toward the library.

Phoebe considered this. "He's okay. He'd look better if he didn't have to wear those glasses."

"Fee! I was talking about Chip!"

"Oh. I didn't really notice."

Linn poked Jessica. "I think Fee's got a crush on Leonard."

"Don't be ridiculous," Phoebe said. "I just think he's intelligent, that's all. We were having a very interesting conversation."

"*Sure,* Fee," Linn said knowingly.

"Isn't everything perfect?" Jessica sighed. "You and Chip. Me and Tommy. Fee and Leonard. Now we just have to find someone for Melanie."

Phoebe didn't even bother to respond to this. She was thinking about something else.

The girls left her at the library, and Phoebe went inside. Ms. Wrenn was in her office, flipping through some magazines.

"What are you doing?" Phoebe asked.

"I'm looking up reviews of all the Betsy Drake books. If I'm going to have to defend these books in front of the town council, I'd better gather some ammunition."

Phoebe perched on the edge of the desk. "I don't get it, Ms. Wrenn. Do you really think those books are so great?"

Ms. Wrenn looked up. "They're good books, Fee. *You* may not like them, and that's your privilege, but a lot of other kids are crazy about them. But that's not even the point. . . ."

She'd said that before, but Phoebe didn't know what she meant. "What's the point, then?"

Ms. Wrenn sat down. "It's the principle of the thing. People don't have the right to make those kinds of choices for other people. Mrs. Lane and her companions are saying they want to decide what all kids will be able to read. You're intelligent enough to make your own decisions about what you read, aren't you?"

"Sure."

"Well, it's my job to protect the rights of all you kids to read what you want to read and to make your own choices. And not let other people interfere with that process."

"What do those people think is so terrible about these books, anyway?"

Ms. Wrenn looked thoughtful. "Well, you know what Betsy Drake writes about—the problems girls and boys have when they become adolescents, such as dealing with changing bodies, new ideas, that sort of thing."

"Daphne told me about one she read last year about a girl who was worried because she didn't have her period and all the other girls in her class did. But then it turned out half the other girls were lying."

Ms. Wrenn nodded. "Yes, that's one of the books Mrs. Lane was most upset about. She thinks kids your age are too young to be reading about things like that."

"Why?" Phoebe was indignant. "That's real-life stuff!"

"Of course it is! But some people think kids should be protected from the realities of life."

"That's dumb," Phoebe muttered. Who did those people think they were, anyway? "You're not going to let them get away with it, are you?"

Ms. Wrenn sighed. "I'm going to try not to . . . but it won't be easy. Especially if Mrs. Lane drums up a lot of support."

"Why don't you get people to help you?" Phoebe asked.

"I'd like to, Fee. But it's not easy getting people involved. Most adults think kids' books aren't that important an issue." She shook her head. "You kids are really the ones who would suffer from this."

Phoebe had an inspiration. "Then we're the ones who should help you! I'll call all my friends and tell them about this!"

Ms. Wrenn looked a little perturbed. "Wait a minute, Fee. If people think I've organized you kids to protest, they might think I'm using my influence on you. To tell you the truth, I could get into some real trouble."

"Oh." Phoebe felt deflated.

Ms. Wrenn patted her on the shoulder. "But I appreciate your support. Look, why don't you get these books together for the story hour while I search for reviews of Betsy Drake books?"

"Okay." Phoebe took the list from her and started out of the room. Then she paused at the door, frowning.

"It's sort of like cheese fishburgers, isn't it?"

"What?"

"I mean, I think cheese fishburgers are pretty disgusting. But Leonard's got a right to eat them if he wants to."

Ms. Wrenn looked at her blankly. "Phoebe, what are you talking about?"

But Phoebe didn't hear her. Lost in her own thoughts, she wandered out to the shelves.

9

STILL IN HER PAJAMAS and slippers, Phoebe shuffled down to the kitchen the next morning. Daphne was already at the table, absentmindedly eating a bowl of cereal while her real attention was focused on a book. Mrs. Gray was on the phone.

"No, Shirley, I haven't had a chance to read any of those books. What's that one about?" There was a pause.

"Shocked? No. Books for kids have changed a lot since we were young. They're much more realistic." There was another pause.

"No, I don't think it sounds trashy. In fact, I'm rather impressed. I think it's healthy for kids to read about—" She didn't get a chance to finish her sentence, and Phoebe saw her flinch. Mrs. Lane must be offering her opinion loudly.

"Shirley, I have *four* daughters! Of course I'm concerned about their well-being. I just don't see how a book like that can hurt them!"

Phoebe poured herself some cereal, but her eyes stayed on her mother's face. Mrs. Gray was getting "the look."

"Shirley, I'd love to talk with you some more about this, but right now I'm more concerned with the fact that my youngest is about to pour cereal all over the kitchen floor. No, I can't support you on this. I'm sorry, but I do think *my* girls are old enough to handle their own reading."

She emphasized the words *my girls.* Phoebe wondered if that included her. Somehow, she doubted it.

Mrs. Gray hung up the phone and groaned. "That woman," she muttered, half under her breath. "What a narrow mind."

"Why did you call her?" Phoebe asked.

"I didn't," her mother said, glancing at the clock while she began clearing the table. "She called me. She's trying to get everyone to come to the town council meeting on Tuesday to support her. Daphne, would you please put that book down and finish your breakfast? I swear, sometimes you're like a baby the way you dawdle."

Daphne looked up vaguely. "Huh? Oh, sure, Mom."

"Honestly," Mrs. Gray murmured, "I don't know how you kids are going to manage once I start teaching. I feel like I'm leaving behind a house full of infants."

Phoebe glanced at Daphne to see how she was reacting to this. But Daphne seemed unconcerned. She was consuming her cereal rapidly, taking only an occasional furtive peek at the book.

So her mother thought Daphne was a baby, too. That gave Phoebe some small comfort.

"I'm going over to the high school to help with student advising. Cassie! Lydia! Are you ready?"

A voice drifted downstairs. "We're coming!"

"Are they going with you?" Phoebe asked.

"I'm dropping them at the junior high. They've got their registration today. Do you want to be dropped off at the library?"

"No," Phoebe sighed. "Ms. Wrenn says I have to take a day off. She says she could be arrested for breaking child labor laws. Mom, what are you going to do about Mrs. Lane?"

Her mother was checking through the contents of her briefcase. "What?"

"Ms. Wrenn told me that if she doesn't have a lot of support, Mrs. Lane and her friends might convince the town council to ban those books. So what are you going to do?"

Mrs. Gray snapped the briefcase shut. "Fee, I don't know if there's anything I *can* do. I just don't have the time to get involved in this. I'm very busy right now. To tell you the truth, I'm not even sure if I can make it to that town council meeting." She must have caught the look of dismay on Phoebe's face. "Honey, don't get so worried about this. I'm sure somebody will help Ms. Wrenn."

"Help Ms. Wrenn do what?" Lydia sauntered into the kitchen.

"Where's Cassie?" Mrs. Gray demanded.

"She's still getting dressed. She can't decide what to wear."

Mrs. Gray looked like she was about to explode. "That child," she mumbled to herself as she hurried out of the room.

"What were you saying about Ms. Wrenn?" Lydia asked Phoebe.

Phoebe stirred her cereal and milk into mush, the way she liked it. "She told me Mrs. Lane and her friends are going to the town council meeting on Tuesday to get the Betsy Drake books banned from the library."

Lydia uttered a short whistle. "Wow, she really means business, doesn't she!"

"Well, I don't think it's right," Phoebe said.

Lydia looked at her curiously. "I thought you said you didn't even like those books."

"I don't." She recalled what Ms. Wrenn had said. "It's the principle of the thing."

"What are you going to do about it?"

Phoebe shrugged. "I can't do anything. Ms. Wrenn said if people thought she got us kids involved, she might get in trouble." She noticed with some apprehension that her sister's eyes were taking on a familiar glint.

"Well, she didn't tell *me* that. And I bet I could think of something—"

"No way!" Phoebe yelled. Her voice was even louder than she'd intended it to be. Daphne actually looked up from her book.

Lydia blinked. "Why not?"

Phoebe scowled. "This is my problem, not yours. *I'll* think of something."

"But you just said—"

"I'm going to talk to Ms. Wrenn again," Phoebe was surprised to hear herself say. Was that what she was going to do?

"Okay, but you still might need some help. No offense, but you're just a little kid. What do you know about staging a major protest?"

Phoebe made a valiant effort to keep her voice at a normal pitch. "I don't need your help, thank you very much," she said, with what she hoped was exactly the right amount of sarcasm. "I can handle this myself."

Lydia threw up her arms. "Okay, have it your way."

Mrs. Gray returned, dragging a distressed Cassie by one arm.

"But, Mom," her sister was wailing, "I haven't put on my ankle bracelet!"

"Don't worry," Lydia reassured her. "They'll let you register without one." The three of them left by the kitchen door, leaving Phoebe alone with Daphne.

Daphne had closed her book. "Why won't you let Lydia help you? She's good at that kind of thing."

Phoebe shifted uncomfortably. "I don't know. I guess 'cause she'd try to take over. I want to do something myself."

"What are you going to do?"

"I don't know."

"Maybe you could write a letter to the town council," Daphne suggested.

"Maybe," Phoebe replied without much enthusiasm. Somehow, she didn't think a letter would be much ammunition against Mrs. Lane and her friends.

"If I think of anything I'll let you know," Daphne

promised, carrying her cereal dish to the sink. "I've gotta get dressed and go over to Annie's."

Alone, Phoebe put her head in her hands and tried to think. But her mind was like an empty blackboard with no chalk. Finally, she went to the phone and started to dial. Linn used to come up with neat ideas and plans—before she got weird. Maybe if she could take her mind off Chip for a minute . . .

"Hi, it's me."

"Hi! You must have ESP—I was just getting ready to call you. Want to go to the pool?"

"No, I want you to come over here."

"Aw, c'mon," Linn wheedled. "Leonard might be there."

Phoebe groaned. "Linn, I've got something important to tell you."

"Why can't we talk at the pool?"

Phoebe could just imagine trying to tell Linn about the library problem while her friend was flirting with Chip. "I can't. Look, can you come over on your way home?"

"I guess. What's so important? Can't you tell me now?"

It would be hard enough trying to convince Linn to help her in person. She didn't want to chance it over the phone. "No. I'll see you later, okay?"

She hung up and ran upstairs to get dressed. Daphne was still in the room, tying the laces on her sneakers.

"I have an idea," Daphne said.

"Yeah? What?"

"Couldn't Ms. Wrenn just hide the books so Mrs.

Lane wouldn't know they were still there? And if kids wanted to check them out, Ms. Wrenn could just get them."

Phoebe shook her head. "That wouldn't work. What if Mrs. Lane found more and more books she wanted to get rid of? Ms. Wrenn could end up hiding the whole library!"

"I suppose so." Daphne sighed. "Maybe Mom and Dad can do something. I'll see you later."

She didn't understand, Phoebe thought as she got dressed. Lydia was probably the only one who could understand why Phoebe would want to do something herself. But she didn't want Lydia's help. Lydia was the one who had told her to grow up. And she was going to show Lydia that baby Phoebe could act just as grown-up as she did.

With a firm sense of resolution, she left the house and headed toward the library. She had told Lydia she was going to talk to Ms. Wrenn again, and that was exactly what she'd do.

The librarian had just finished a story hour when Phoebe entered the children's room.

"Fee, what are you doing here today? I thought I told you to take the day off."

"I'm not going to work," Phoebe assured her. "I just had to talk to you about something."

"This sounds serious," Ms. Wrenn said. "Come on into my office."

Phoebe followed her in. She noticed a stack of Betsy Drake books on the desk. "Are you taking them off the shelves so kids can't check them out?"

"Good heavens, no!" Ms. Wrenn exclaimed. "I've just been rereading them."

"How come?"

"I wanted to refresh my memory. If I'm going to defend them at the town council meeting, I'd better know my books, don't you think?"

Phoebe sat down. "That's what I wanted to talk to you about." She took a deep breath. "I know you said you couldn't let me get involved because people might think you told me to. But the thing is, I think I ought to do something. I mean, it's not right, what Mrs. Lane and those people want to do . . . is it?"

Ms. Wrenn shook her head slowly. "I don't think it's right."

Encouraged, Phoebe continued. "And you said it was us kids who suffer when people try to take away our books, right?"

Ms. Wrenn nodded.

"Then I want to do something about it," Phoebe declared.

"Like what?"

"Well, I was wondering if you have any ideas."

Ms. Wrenn sighed. "I can't tell you what to do, Fee. I appreciate your feelings, but if I told you what to do, I'd be doing exactly what I said I couldn't do—I'd be using my influence on you."

Phoebe felt as if she'd been reprimanded. "I was only trying to help."

"I know, Fee," Ms. Wrenn said briskly, "and I'm glad to have your support. Now I have to get ready for a meeting."

Phoebe got up and started toward the door.

"Fee," Ms. Wrenn said suddenly, "have you actually read all the Betsy Drake books?"

"I started one once."

Ms. Wrenn picked up the stack on her desk and offered them to her. "Maybe you'd better read them if you're serious about defending them."

Phoebe eyed the books with some distaste but took them. Then something Ms. Wrenn had just said suddenly clicked.

"If I get an idea on my own, something I could do to keep them in the library, would you mind?"

Ms. Wrenn smiled. "Fee, I have faith in you, and I know you won't do anything silly or childish. But if you want to take a stand on this, that's your privilege." Her smile widened. "Like you said, it's a free country."

Phoebe grinned. A few minutes later, lugging the books home, she thought that at least she now had Ms. Wrenn's permission. But for what?

Luckily, the books were pretty easy reading and she was a fast reader. Phoebe had just started the second one when her mother stuck her head into the room.

"What are you reading?" Mrs. Gray asked.

"It's a Betsy Drake book."

"Oh, really?" Her mother came in and picked up one of the books off the bed. "How is it?"

"Okay, I guess. I don't know why people think they're so bad. I mean, they're not dirty. Not like those movies—"

"What movies?"

98

"Oh, nothing." Phoebe began to study the page intently.

"*What* movies?" her mother asked again.

Phoebe gave a weak grin. "Well, once I was at Melanie's, and they have cable TV, and we found this station . . ."

Mrs. Gray raised her eyebrows. "And you watched it?"

"Just a little," Phoebe explained quickly. "It was really gross. Anyway, these books aren't gross like that. I mean, there's this one kid and she talks about sex, but she doesn't do anything. Mostly it's about how she's worried because she isn't developing as fast as her friends."

Mrs. Gray sat down on the bed and looked at Phoebe with concern. "Do you worry about that?"

Phoebe shook her head vigorously. "*I* don't. But some kids talk about it all the time. Like Linn and Melanie and Jessica. I guess that's why they like these books."

Her mother flipped through the book. "I wish I had time to read these. Maybe once school starts and I'm feeling more organized."

"By then, they might not even be in the library anymore," Phoebe said. "If those town council people do what Mrs. Lane tells them to."

"Oh, I doubt that will happen," Mrs. Gray said. "Ms. Wrenn's an excellent librarian, and she'll present the other side of the issue."

"But there's only one of her," Phoebe argued. "Mrs. Lane has all these people on her side. I want to do something to help."

"That's sweet of you, honey, and I'm sure Ms. Wrenn appreciates it," her mother replied, glancing at her watch. "Oh—look at the time! I've got to get to the bookstore before it closes." She gave Phoebe an absent-minded squeeze and left the room.

Great, Phoebe thought. No one was taking her seriously. She looked over at the clock by her bed. It was after four—Linn should be coming any minute. She decided to take her book outside to the front steps and wait for her.

From the hallway she could see Lydia through the slightly opened door to her room. She was lying on the bed, reading. For a second, Phoebe was almost tempted to go in. But then she pushed the thought firmly from her mind.

She had just settled down on the front steps when Linn's mother's car pulled up. She jumped up, expecting to see Linn get out, maybe with Jessica. Her heart sank when she saw Linn emerge with Chip and Leonard.

"Surprise!" Linn called to her happily as the three of them approached the house. "Look who I brought!"

What was she supposed to do, jump up and down for joy? Well, she couldn't be rude. "Hi," she said. "C'mon in."

Linn and Chip went on ahead, but Leonard paused to see what she was reading. "Oh, I read that book," he said.

Phoebe was surprised. "You read a Betsy Drake book? But they're for girls!"

Leonard adjusted his glasses. "There's no law that says boys can't read them."

"But why would any boy want to read these books?"

Phoebe pressed as they went inside. "They're about girl stuff."

Chip, sitting on the couch and looking a little bored, perked up at this. "What girl stuff?"

"We were talking about Betsy Drake," Phoebe explained.

"Who's Betsy Drake?"

"She's an author," Linn told him. "She writes books about . . . uh . . . about things girls talk about."

"Oh, yeah? Like what?"

Linn began to blush furiously. Phoebe wasn't particularly comfortable either, but she figured Chip deserved an answer. "Well, you know, sort of like . . . um . . . things that happen to girls when they're . . . uh . . . growing up."

Chip looked blank. And then he went a little pink. "Oh."

Leonard nodded seriously. "That's why I read them. So I can know more about girls."

Phoebe looked at him with respect. That was actually a very sensible thing to do. She wondered briefly if Betsy Drake had written any books about boys.

"Anyway, that's what I wanted to talk to Linn about. You see, there are some people who think Betsy Drake's books shouldn't be in the library, because they're so, you know, realistic. And they're going to the town council meeting on Tuesday to get them to tell the library to get rid of them. And I want to do something about it."

"Why?" Linn asked. "You can buy them in paperback."

"That's not the point," Phoebe said. "It's not right for

them to do that! It's like they're saying we're babies and we're not old enough to choose our own books. And I don't think we should let them get away with it."

"Neither do I," Leonard joined in. Now *he* was looking at *her* with respect. "It's un-American to tell people what they can read."

"But we're not just people," Linn argued. "I mean, we're kids."

Phoebe turned to her in frustration. "So what? We still have rights . . . I think. Anyway, it's not like we're little kids. I mean, you're already wearing a—"

"Fee!" Linn shrieked.

Chip was looking at her with interest. "You're already wearing a what?"

"Like I was saying," Phoebe said hurriedly, trying to avoid Linn's eyes, "we ought to do something about this."

"Like what?" Leonard asked.

Phoebe made a helpless gesture. "I don't know. I thought maybe Linn might come up with something."

Linn's face had almost returned to its normal color. "Gee, I don't know. I don't think there's anything we can do."

"Of course there is," Phoebe said spiritedly. When no one responded, she looked over at Leonard. "Isn't there?"

"There must be," Leonard said. He turned to Chip. "What she's saying is right. Freedom to read is just as important as—"

"Freedom to eat cheese fishburgers," Phoebe supplied. Leonard nodded in approval.

Chip just shrugged. "Look, I don't care. I don't read all that much anyway."

Leonard faced him sternly. His glasses slid down his nose but he ignored them. "What if somebody decided to get rid of soccer? Nobody could play soccer anymore. What would you think of that?"

Chip's eyes narrowed. "I'd like to see 'em try."

"Well, it's the same thing," Leonard said. "Some people don't like soccer. But they don't have the right to tell other people they can't play."

"Exactly!" Phoebe said.

"What we've gotta do," Leonard continued, "is figure out how to handle this in a mature sort of way. So people won't treat us like little kids."

Phoebe beamed at him. Who would ever have thought a boy could understand what she was talking about?

Chip didn't seem particularly convinced, but at least Linn was showing a spark of interest.

"I was just thinking," she said slowly. "If we did something about this and my mother thought I was being really mature, she might let me start wearing mascara."

Phoebe rolled her eyes. Linn *would* have an ulterior motive. But she didn't say anything. No matter what the reason, at least she had one more person on her side.

"But what are we going to do?" Phoebe asked, for what seemed like the zillionth time.

"I think we need some help," Leonard said slowly. "Somebody who knows about this kind of thing. Do any of you guys know anyone who's done anything like this?

You know, like been in protests or demonstrations?"

A car was honking outside.

"That's my mother," Linn said, getting up. "She said she'd pick us up on the way back from the store. C'mon, guys."

"But you can't leave yet," Phoebe exclaimed in dismay. "We haven't come up with any ideas!"

At least Leonard looked apologetic. "I have to get home for dinner. But I'll keep thinking about it."

"You'll come up with something," Linn assured her. "We'll help you."

Sure, Phoebe thought, while you're deciding what color mascara to get.

The car was honking again. "We've gotta go," Linn said. "See ya later, Fee."

They all ran out, leaving Phoebe standing there without an idea in the world. So they were going to help her. Help her do what?

But something Leonard had said kept ringing in her ears. They needed help—help from someone who knew what this was all about.

And Phoebe knew what she had to do. Pride was important, but they were getting desperate. She left the room, marched upstairs, and pushed open the door to the room where her oldest sister lay reading.

"Lydia?"

She looked up from her book. "Yeah?"

Phoebe smiled weakly.

"Help."

10

No MATTER WHAT the problem is, it never seems quite as bad in the morning. Phoebe knew this when she opened her eyes to bright sunlight streaming in the window and her oldest sister leaning against her door.

"Okay, out of bed! If you're going to save the world's kids from Mrs. Lane, you'd better get started."

Phoebe promptly rubbed the sleep from her eyes and jumped out of bed. In the twin bed next to hers, Daphne sat up and gazed at Lydia in awe.

"Are you really going to try to stop Mrs. Lane?"

Lydia shook her head. "This is Fee's adventure. I'm just along for the ride." She turned to Phoebe, who was quickly pulling on her jeans. "Meet you downstairs in five minutes."

Phoebe was down in three. Lydia was perusing the Betsy Drake books. She looked up when Phoebe entered the room, wearing an expression the whole family had come to recognize—eyes flashing, cheeks flushed, and the general appearance of a soldier prepared to do battle.

"I love a good fight," she said happily. Something in Phoebe's face made her hastily add, "Okay, okay, I know, it's *your* fight. But I can still enjoy it, can't I?"

Phoebe grinned and nodded. To be honest, she wasn't really worried that Lydia might take over. As nervous as she felt about this whole business, she was glad to see someone exuding confidence.

Lydia waved her hand at the books on the table. "Look, if Mrs. Lane and her buddies are convinced that these books are trash, you're probably not going to change their minds. I mean, taste is a subjective thing, right?"

Phoebe wasn't sure what her sister meant, but it sounded good. "Right."

"So we—I mean, you—should just forget all about Mrs. Lane and concentrate on the town council members and the other people who come to the meeting. You want to convince them that these books are okay for kids your age to read."

"How?"

"Well, what do you think of the books?" With her pen poised on an open notebook, Lydia looked at her expectantly.

Phoebe pondered this. "I tried one a few months ago, but I didn't like it. I mean, I just didn't think it was interesting. I didn't even finish it. But yesterday I read two of them, all the way through. I'm still not crazy about them. I guess I'm just not all that interested in the stuff that goes on—you know, all these girls worrying about some boy liking them, or whether they'll ever get their period."

Lydia frowned. "If you tell the town council that, they'll just think Mrs. Lane is right."

But Phoebe wasn't finished. "The strange thing is, though, after I read those books, I sort of understood why Linn and Jess and Mel have been acting so different. I mean, I can see that it's all sort of natural. It doesn't seem so weird anymore."

"That's good," Lydia said, writing something down. Phoebe leaned over to see it.

" 'Betsy Drake's books help kids understand what growing up is all about,' " she read aloud.

"Now, what else can you say about them?" Lydia asked.

"I don't know," Phoebe replied. "They're very popular. Everyone I know reads them."

Lydia brightened. "Hey—I think you just hit on something there."

Phoebe was confused. "Huh?"

"If these books are so popular, then lots of kids should be interested in this." She got up and started pacing around the room. "We need support. There's strength in numbers. United we stand, and all that."

"What are you *talking* about?"

Lydia finally stood still. "You're going to get on the phone and call all your friends. We're going to create a real show of support at that town council meeting."

Phoebe was puzzled. "You mean I should just get a bunch of kids to show up at the town council meeting? What good will that do?"

"You won't just be sitting there. You're going to do something."

"Like what? Make faces at Mrs. Lane? Throw paper airplanes?" At the sight of Lydia's face, she quickly added, "Just kidding."

"Dummy, the whole point of this is to show how you're old enough to choose your own books. If you act like little kids, they'll believe everything Mrs. Lane says. You've gotta be *mature*."

"I *said* I was kidding."

"Okay, okay. Do you have a list of all the kids who were in your class last year?"

"Yeah, I think it's still on the bulletin board in the kitchen." She got up to get it, but eyed Lydia uneasily. "Are you saying I've got to call all these kids?"

"Not all of them," Lydia said cheerfully. "Just enough to look like a mob."

Phoebe returned with the list. "What should I tell them?"

Lydia thought for a moment. "Don't say too much," she said finally. "Be a little mysterious. Just tell them something very important's going on, and you want them to meet you this afternoon."

"Meet me where?"

"What's going on?" Mrs. Gray asked, catching their last words as she came into the room. Phoebe looked at Lydia, but her sister just shrugged.

"This is *your* thing. *You* tell her."

Mrs. Gray looked at them suspiciously. "Tell me what?"

Phoebe explained. "I'm going to call some kids from my class and ask them to come over to talk about this Betsy Drake thing." She glanced at Lydia again, but her sister was gazing at the ceiling. "We're thinking maybe we should go to this town council meeting."

"And do what?"

Phoebe shifted her weight from one foot to the other. "Uh, we don't know yet. But it'll be something, uh, mature."

Worry lines etched Mrs. Gray's forehead. "Lydia, what have you gotten her into?"

"It's not my fault," Lydia said innocently. "This is all Fee's idea. I'm just hanging around as a sort of advisor."

"Is it okay if I ask the kids to come here?" Phoebe broke in.

"I suppose so. I won't be home, though. I'm going to my new women's group meeting this afternoon."

Lydia looked at her with interest. "What women's group?"

Mrs. Gray perched on the edge of the sofa. "It's something new. It's a group of women about my age who are going back to work after being home for a long time. We're planning to meet monthly to talk about the difficulties, the experiences, how going back to work is changing our lives—that sort of thing."

Phoebe examined her mother. It wasn't just the hair that was making her look different lately. There was something else.

"You're really happy about teaching, aren't you, Mom?"

Her mother nodded. "I feel like I'm going into another phase of my life. It's a little scary, but it's exciting."

Lydia nodded. "I think it's great, Mom! I don't think people should ever stop changing and growing."

Slowly, Phoebe nodded too. Changing, growing. Like Linn and Melanie and Jessica. Like the girls in Betsy Drake's books. Was she changing and growing, too? She wasn't sure . . . but she didn't have time to worry about it now.

Her mother's worry lines had returned. "Now you've gotten me to change the subject. Tell me more about what you kids are planning to do at this meeting this afternoon."

There wasn't any more to tell yet, but Phoebe tried. "We're getting kids together to decide how we're going to fight Mrs. Lane."

Mrs. Gray made a face. "Don't say *fight*, Fee. It sounds so . . . aggressive. How about *challenge*?"

"Okay," Phoebe said agreeably.

But her mother still looked concerned. "I just don't want to see you get in over your head, honey. This is pretty serious business."

"Fee can handle it," Lydia said with enough confidence for the both of them.

Mrs. Gray looked at them doubtfully. "You're not planning anything . . . *violent*, are you?"

Lydia laughed. "Like bopping Mrs. Lane on the head with Betsy Drake books?"

Now who was acting like a little kid? Phoebe patted

her mother's arm. "Don't worry, Mom. We won't do anything to embarrass you."

Her mother's face softened. "Darling, you couldn't do anything that would embarrass me." She paused, and then in another tone added, "Could you?"

"C'mon, we've gotta make these calls," Lydia announced.

Mrs. Gray gazed affectionately at her daughters. "My two little revolutionaries," she murmured. Shaking her head in amazement, she left the room.

"Start with this one," Lydia said, indicating the name at the top of the roster.

Phoebe looked at the list. "Gina Allston. I hardly know her." She took the list and Lydia followed her into the kitchen.

Tentatively, Phoebe dialed the first number.

"Uh, could I speak to Gina, please?"

"This is Gina."

"Oh, hi, Gina. This is Phoebe Gray, from school."

She could picture her quiet, meek-looking classmate's puzzled expression.

"Oh, hello, Phoebe."

Phoebe spoke the next words in a rush. "Look, Gina, there's something going on at the public library that's very serious and very important and it affects all the kids our age. And I'm asking a bunch of kids to come over here this afternoon at two."

Gina sounded definitely curious. "What's it all about?"

Phoebe paused. Would Gina even be familiar with Betsy Drake's books? If anyone in the class was even less grown up than Phoebe, it was Gina. She still wore little-girl dresses and her mother showed up at school every afternoon to walk her home.

"Well, some people are trying to have books banned from the children's room, and we're trying to come up with a way to stop them."

"What books?"

"Have you ever heard of Betsy Drake?"

Gina's normally soft voice rose slightly. "Sure! I just started reading her books this summer. They're neat!"

Phoebe tried to keep the surprise out of her voice. "Well, those are the books they're trying to ban."

"No way! I'll be there!"

"Great!"

Phoebe hung up the phone and turned to Lydia excitedly. "She's coming!"

Lydia grinned approvingly. "Now call this one."

Phoebe checked the name and frowned. "Mimi Barnes. She's that snotty rich kid who's always saying she's going to transfer to a private school."

"Rich kids read, too. Call her!"

Phoebe dialed.

"Barnes residence."

"May I speak to Mimi, please?"

She heard the person who answered call for "Miss Mimi" and rolled her eyes. Then Mimi was on the line. Quickly, Phoebe explained her purpose in calling.

"And if we don't stop this, we won't be able to check any Betsy Drake books out of the library."

"I don't use the library. I buy all my own books."

"Oh." Phoebe was about to say good-bye and hang up, but Mimi went on.

"I don't have anything to do this afternoon, though. So maybe I'll come. It's better than sitting around at home."

After hanging up, Phoebe related the brief conversation to Lydia. "She isn't really interested."

Lydia shrugged. "It doesn't matter. The more warm bodies, the better. Keep calling. The more kids we get, the more powerful we'll look."

Just as Phoebe reached for the phone, it rang. Startled, Phoebe let it ring again before answering it.

"Fee? Hi—it's me. Wait till you hear this." Linn wasn't even going to give her a chance to say hello. "I couldn't believe it. This morning, I went to the library and I got the new Betsy Drake book out and I brought it home. My mother saw it, and she says I can't read it till she finds out what all the fuss is about. She's even going to that town council meeting!"

"See, I told you this was important!" Phoebe said. Then she told her friend about the meeting that afternoon.

"I'll be there," Linn promised. "And I'll bring Jess. And I'll call Mel and see if she's talked her way out of being grounded yet. Can I bring Chip?"

"Sure," Phoebe replied. "And tell him to call Leonard, okay?"

"Aha! I knew you liked him!"

"C'mon," Lydia pressed, tapping her foot impatiently. "You've got a lot more calls to make."

Hastily, Phoebe finished the conversation. Then she continued making calls. A lot of kids were still away on summer vacations, but she managed to get hold of three more.

"That's eight girls," she told Lydia, "plus Chip and Leonard. Think that's enough?"

"You want to call more boys?"

Phoebe wrinkled her nose. "Not if I don't have to. If you get too many boys together in one place, they start acting goofy."

"Yeah, I know what you mean. Okay, I guess that's enough."

Phoebe looked at the clock. "They're going to be here in two hours. What are you going to tell them?"

"You mean, what are *you* going to tell them."

Right, Phoebe thought. Why did her insides suddenly feel like bubbling mush?

Lydia was beaming at her. "You're in charge of this, Fee! Remember that!"

I'm in charge, Phoebe repeated to herself two hours later as she stood in the living room surveying the scene. Kids were talking, laughing, settling themselves on the sofa and the chairs and the floor.

Lydia was roaming among them with a stack of paper cups and a pitcher of lemonade. She'd even coaxed Daphne into the group—she was following Lydia with a tray of hastily baked cookies. When she passed Phoebe, she whispered, "I won't have to talk or anything, will I?" Phoebe assured her she wouldn't.

But Phoebe *was* going to have to talk. And even with all the chatter, the slurping, the chewing going on, she thought for sure everyone could hear her heart pounding.

There's nothing to worry about, she told herself sternly. These are just kids—your friends. There was

Linn, sitting in the corner next to Chip, who was looking distinctly uncomfortable with all these girls around. Jessica was next to them, looking a little glum. Maybe she'd tried to get Tommy to come and he couldn't. Phoebe was glad. Even though he would have been one more warm body, she didn't think Dracula impersonations would go over big at the town council.

And Melanie was there too, looking especially cheerful—probably because she'd talked her way out of being grounded again. Leonard sat comfortably on an easy chair, drinking his lemonade, eating his cookie, and pausing every few minutes to push back his glasses. He looked like being one of only two boys in a crowd of girls was the most natural thing in the world.

Phoebe took a deep breath. "Uh, the reason I asked you all to come here—" she began, and then stopped. No one was listening.

"Listen, guys," she tried again, a little louder. They were still talking. She looked frantically at Lydia, who was perched on the arm of the sofa.

"Hey!" Lydia yelled sharply. Everyone stopped whatever they were doing and stared at her. "Phoebe's got something to tell you."

There was something about Lydia's voice that made all eyes turn obediently to Phoebe. Sometimes it paid to have a sister who took charge. Phoebe took another deep breath.

"I told you guys what this was about on the phone. Some people want to take all the Betsy Drake books out of the library. Ms. Wrenn, the librarian, told them the library wouldn't do it. So these people are going to the town council meeting on Tuesday to get the books banned."

"What do they want to do that for?" one of the girls asked.

"Because they think the books have stuff in them we shouldn't be reading. Stuff like . . ." She closed her eyes. She couldn't believe she was about to say this in front of boys. "Stuff like menstruation."

She opened her eyes. Chip had his mouth open. Leonard's expression hadn't changed at all.

Melanie's face was screwed up. "But that's what happens! Why shouldn't we read about it?"

"Because they think we're not old enough."

Mimi Barnes spoke. "That's stupid." A rumble of agreement went through the room.

"What's Ms. Wrenn going to do?" Gina Allston asked.

"She's going to defend the books at the meeting, and tell everyone how good they are and all that. But since we're the ones who read the books, I think we should go to the meeting, too, and support her."

"How?" Jessica asked.

How. That was the big question.

"Well, that's why I asked you guys to come here," Phoebe said. "So we can figure out something we can do."

The room fell silent as everyone digested this.

"Wait a minute," Leonard said slowly. "I think I've got an idea."

All eyes turned to him expectantly.

"If they think we're too young to read these books, we just have to show them we're not."

"But *how*?" Phoebe asked urgently.

"We'll tell them," Leonard said simply.

Phoebe thought about this. And then she started to get excited. "We could get up at the meeting, one at a time, and tell them why we should be allowed to read these books."

"Exactly," Leonard said.

Jessica spoke in a quavering voice. "You mean we have to get up in front of the whole town council? And all the other people?"

"I went to one of those meetings once with my parents," another girl said. "They have these microphones in the aisles." She shivered. "Your voice booms out really loud."

Now everyone was exchanging nervous looks. Daphne had actually gone white.

"We don't all have to do it," Phoebe said quickly.

Lydia spoke up. "Five or six are plenty. If there are too many of you talking, they'll just get bored."

Phoebe shot her a grateful look. "Okay, who wants to talk?" She raised her own hand. Leonard raised his. No one else did.

"C'mon, you guys! There's nothing to be afraid of!" Resolutely, she pushed out of her mind the image of herself standing at a microphone talking to a bunch of grown-ups. She couldn't ask others to do it if she wasn't prepared to do it herself—but the mere thought was making her feel queasy.

They all exchanged uneasy looks. No one raised a hand.

"Linn," Phoebe said, "you're the one who likes these books so much."

Linn at least had the decency to look sheepish for a

moment. Phoebe fixed her eyes on her. C'mon, Linn, she thought urgently. We're Doodlebugs! We're in this together! And when Linn didn't respond to mental telepathy, her lips silently formed the word *mascara*.

She couldn't be sure if her friend had caught that. But it didn't matter. Linn raised her hand.

Phoebe sighed in relief. "That's three."

"I have to ask my mother," Gina said shyly. "But maybe I can . . ."

"Good," Phoebe said. "That's four."

And then she saw Melanie poke Jessica. Two more hands went up.

"Six!" Phoebe cried happily. "Now the rest of you still have to come to the meeting."

"Why?" Mimi asked.

"Because . . . because . . ." She looked at Lydia.

"To provide moral support," Lydia supplied promptly. "To let everyone know whose side you're on."

Chip looked up with interest. "Like, we could cheer and clap and whistle when you guys talk, and when the other guys talk we could boo."

That was the longest sentence Phoebe had ever heard him say. She grinned at him until she realized Lydia was frowning.

"No, don't do that," her sister said sharply. "You're trying to show these people how mature you are, that you're not a bunch of babies. If you start yelling, they'll probably just throw you out."

Chip's face fell.

"Well, maybe a little applause will be okay," Lydia conceded. "But no booing."

"How do we get the town council to let us talk?" Linn asked.

Phoebe looked at Lydia.

Her sister stood up. Phoebe wasn't at all sorry to see her "take charge" expression.

"You want to do this in an organized way. First, Phoebe should call the town council secretary to get yourselves on the agenda." She paused. "It'll be too confusing if she gives all your names. You need a good group name."

The room fell silent as the girls pondered this. Then Jessica piped up. "How about Books R Us?"

Lydia shook her head. "Too cute. You want something that sounds serious. We're talking about your rights here, the freedom to read what you want to read."

"I've got it!" Phoebe exclaimed. "How about the Right to Read Club?"

"Or the Right to Read Society?" Mimi suggested. "That sounds more elegant."

There was a general murmur of agreement. Phoebe's mind was racing. "Okay, so when they call on us, I'll get up and say how we're here to support these books. Then I'll call on each of you, one at a time, and you'll get up and say what the books mean to you."

"Write it down ahead of time so you won't feel so nervous," Lydia said.

An excited murmur went through the group. Then everyone started talking at once.

"Hey! Listen!" Phoebe yelled. To her amazement, they did.

"Now, we'll all meet at the town council meeting, okay?"

There was a rumble of agreement.

"And dress up," Lydia added. "You want to look mature."

Melanie looked up mischievously. "Does that include you, Fee?"

Phoebe looked down at her too-small T-shirt and jeans patched at the knee. She sighed. "Yeah, I guess I can dig up a skirt."

Still chattering excitedly, the group broke up and the girls started leaving.

"This is a neat idea," Jessica told Phoebe.

"You've really got guts," Linn said admiringly.

"Yeah," Melanie added, "you're good at this!"

"This is the best Doodlebug project you've ever dreamed up," Jessica added. "Even if it's not just Doodlebugs."

Phoebe basked in the praise. "And now you'll get your mascara," she said to Linn.

Linn looked blank. "Huh?"

"The mascara! Isn't that why you said you'd talk at the meeting? So your mother would think you're grown-up enough to wear mascara?"

"Gee," Linn said thoughtfully. "I forgot all about that."

"Well, it looks like Shirley Lane means business," Mr. Gray said as the family convened at the dinner table. "We got a letter from her today at the paper."

"That's okay," Lydia said smugly. "We're ready for her."

Mr. Gray looked at her. "What do you mean?"

Phoebe took over. "We're going to the town council meeting, too. A whole bunch of us."

"Oh, really?" Mr. Gray exchanged glances with Mrs. Gray. "And may I be so bold as to ask what you plan to do there?"

"Oh, we're just going to let people know how we feel," Phoebe replied airily. Then she caught Lydia's eye and burst into giggles.

"I can't believe you're actually going to get up in front of all those people," Daphne murmured. There was awe in her eyes.

Phoebe couldn't quite believe it either.

"What are you talking about?" Cassie demanded.

Phoebe explained. "A bunch of us are planning to go to the meeting to tell the town council that Mrs. Lane and those other people are wrong. We're old enough to read those Betsy Drake books."

Cassie looked aghast. "You're going to argue? With Mrs. Lane?"

"Sure," Phoebe said, hoping she sounded more confident than she felt. "Mrs. Lane is a creep."

Now Cassie's eyes were like saucers. "You're not going to call her that, are you?"

"No . . . but maybe I should."

"You better not," Cassie warned her.

"Why?"

Cassie gave her an exasperated look. "Barbie Lane is just about my best friend. It would be very embarrassing if my own sister called my best friend's mother a creep."

"Fee would never be rude like that," Daphne said loyally. "Would you, Fee?"

"I guess not," Phoebe admitted. "Hey, Dad, will there be a reporter at the meeting?"

"Sure," her father said, still looking puzzled. "We always cover the town council. No matter how boring it is."

"It won't be boring this time," Lydia said gaily.

Mr. Gray turned to his wife. "Do you know what's going on here?"

"I'm not sure," Mrs. Gray said. "But I think we should be prepared for a very interesting meeting."

Daphne smiled proudly. "I think so, too!"

"You better believe it!" Lydia said, looking cocky.

But Cassie's eyes were wary. "Just don't embarrass us."

11

I CAN'T BELIEVE you're really doing this," Daphne said, curled up in the window seat.

Phoebe couldn't see her—the towel covering her freshly washed hair was falling in her face. But the awe and admiration in her sister's voice were unmistakable.

"Aren't you scared?"

"My stomach feels a little funny," Phoebe admitted. She didn't elaborate and add that her head was throbbing and her knees were shaking. And she suspected that the face under the towel was unusually pale.

"I still wish we had made some signs." Lydia was frowning as she sat cross-legged on Phoebe's bed. Even though she had promised she wouldn't do or say anything at the meeting, she was wearing her regulation protest clothes: black jeans, black shirt, and a red bandanna tied across her forehead. Her sisters called it the "don't mess with me" look.

"No way," Phoebe said. "The kids aren't about to carry signs. It was hard enough getting them to agree to talk into those microphones." She'd spent the past two days taking phone calls from anxious classmates begging to be let off, and had been pleasantly surprised to realize how good she was at warding off panic.

"But it could have been a real demonstration if we had had signs," Lydia continued. "We could have marched around the Town Hall before the meeting. It would have freaked out the town council."

Phoebe rolled her eyes. "We don't want to freak them out, Lydia. We just want them to listen."

Daphne grinned. "I think you two have entirely different protest styles."

"What's this about styles?" Cassie asked, entering the room. She was heavily armed—blow dryer in one hand, electric curlers in the other.

"*Protest* styles," Lydia said. "You wouldn't know anything about that."

"Yes, I would," Cassie insisted. "I was in a protest once. Just last year, in fact."

Lydia looked at her with interest. "What kind of protest?"

"Me and four other girls went to the principal's office to complain about the girls' restrooms. The mirrors weren't large enough."

The other sisters exchanged meaningful looks, but Cassie ignored them. She was examining Phoebe critically, her head cocked to one side.

"How do I look?" Phoebe asked, twirling daintily in her oversized quilted robe and tossing her towel-turbaned head.

Cassie pulled the towel off and the stringy wet strands fell in Phoebe's face. "Well, at least it's clean," was her only comment.

Phoebe gazed apprehensively at the equipment Cassie had brought in with her. "What's that for?"

"It's for you," Cassie replied briskly. "If you're going to stand up in front of the entire town council, I don't want you looking like a total nerd. Somebody might recognize you. Someone might know you're my sister. Now sit down and let me get to work on you."

Obediently, Phoebe sat down. With the confidence of a professional beautician, Cassie pulled a brush through Phoebe's hair with one hand while using the other to aim a blast of hot air on it. Usually Phoebe hated being fussed over this way, but this time she found Cassie's attention sort of comforting. In fact, she was enjoying the way everyone seemed to be focusing on her. It seemed like a long time since she'd been the center of attention.

"Now remember," Lydia said loudly, trying to be heard over the blow dryer, "speak strongly and forcibly. Make sure they know you mean business!"

"What?" Phoebe could barely hear her.

"Speak loudly!" Lydia yelled.

"Well, I'm not going to scream," Phoebe said mildly, patting the soft waves that were beginning to appear on her head.

Cassie paused to examine her work. "You know, Fee,

I never realized this before. You have natural curl!" Her eyes were wide, and she looked like she had just made the most remarkable discovery on earth.

Phoebe gazed at her own reflection. How funny—she looked, well, almost pretty!

And she was amazed to hear something that sounded like envy in Cassie's voice when her sister said, "We won't even have to use the electric curlers." Then she went to Phoebe's closet. "Now, let's find something halfway decent for you to wear." She began pushing aside hangers, her nose wrinkling delicately as she perused each item. "Fee! Don't you have anything but jeans and overalls?"

"I think there's a dress in there somewhere," Phoebe said vaguely.

Cassie pulled a dress out of the closet and made a face. "You can't wear this. It'll make you look six years old. Fee, don't you have anything more sophisticated?"

"Wait a minute." Daphne jumped off the window seat and went to her side of the closet. She rummaged a bit, then pulled out a plain white blouse and matching skirt. "How about these?"

Phoebe slipped out of her robe and put on the shirt and skirt. She felt very peculiar—it had been so long since she'd worn a skirt. But one look at her sisters' expressions told her she didn't *look* that way.

"Oh, Fee, you look terrific!" Daphne cried.

"Not bad" was Cassie's judgment. "Not bad at all." And coming from Cassie, that was a major compliment.

Even Lydia was nodding with approval. "Go show Mom and Dad how nice you look."

Feeling jittery and more than a little spacey, Phoebe floated down the hall to her parents' bedroom. The door was closed. She was just about to knock when she heard her own name behind the door.

Phoebe knew she shouldn't eavesdrop, but couldn't resist the temptation and pressed an ear closer to the door.

"Poor baby," her mother was saying. "I just hope she's not too disappointed if this business tonight doesn't work out. She's been so touchy lately."

"Really? I hadn't noticed." That was her father's voice. "Is something wrong?"

"Not really," her mother said. "Just a severe onset of adolescence."

"Oh, c'mon," her father objected. "She's just a baby."

Phoebe could faintly hear her mother's laugh. "I'm not so sure of that."

Neither am I, Phoebe thought. She rapped lightly on the door.

"Come in," her mother called out.

Phoebe opened the door and stood in the entrance-way. Her father, who was in the middle of knotting his tie, practically froze as he took in the picture of his youngest daughter. Her mother clapped her hands together in delight. Then she turned to her husband.

"What did I tell you?"

The steps of the Town Hall were covered with Cedar Park residents pausing to chat before they made their way into the building. As they approached the imposing white building with its massive pillars, Phoebe felt her stomach bounce wildly. What if she got sick? What if she threw up in front of the entire town council? What was she doing here, anyway?

Then she saw Gina Allston, standing beside two adults Phoebe figured were her parents. She was pointing at Phoebe and tugging on her father's arm.

"That's her! She's the one who organized us! Hey, Phoebe!"

Phoebe waved back. Suddenly she felt stronger. Everyone was depending on her.

She and her sisters followed their parents into the building. Phoebe was amazed to see how many more people were already inside.

"Gee, it looks like the whole town's here!"

Her father nodded. "That's because there are some big issues coming up tonight."

Phoebe lifted her head proudly.

Her father continued. "The council's voting on garbage maintenance and alternate side of the street parking."

"Oh."

Her parents were greeting friends. Cassie had darted away to the restroom to check on her hair. Daphne had found her friend Annie and they were talking. Lydia was surveying the room with a professional eye.

"I'm trying to decide if they look hostile," she told Phoebe.

Phoebe saw Mrs. Lane sitting at the front of the large room. She felt her stomach lurch again. Then she spotted Ms. Wrenn sitting on the other side and felt better. She hurried over to her.

"Hi, Ms. Wrenn," she said, eyeing the librarian admiringly. In her tailored beige dress, her briefcase on her lap, she looked every inch the professional, totally confident.

"Fee! Don't you look nice!"

"Well, I figured since I'd be getting up in front of everyone, I'd better dress up. And my sister Cassie didn't want me to embarrass the whole family."

Ms. Wrenn laughed. "Are you on the agenda for the meeting?"

Phoebe nodded. "I told the secretary I represented the Right to Read Society. I thought that sounded very serious." She sighed. "But then she asked me if my mother knew I was calling."

"Well, Phoebe, I have no idea what you kids are planning. I think I've got a pretty good defense of these books worked up, but I can always use some support."

Phoebe felt awkward. "I hope what we're doing is okay. I mean, I hope you don't mind . . ."

"Phoebe, I'm sure anything you've got planned is just fine. You're the kind of patron who makes me proud to be a librarian."

Phoebe felt herself blushing.

"Are you nervous?"

Phoebe patted the pocket of her skirt to make sure her speech was still there. "Oh, no—not at all," she lied.

Ms. Wrenn smiled slightly. "Really? I'm petrified."

For some reason, that made Phoebe feel better.

"I guess I'd better go make sure all the kids are here," she said. She pulled a folded sheet of paper from her pocket and went back up the aisle, letting her eyes scan every row. As she spotted each girl who had attended the library meeting, she waved, flashed a *V* for *Victory* sign, and checked them off on the list. In one row, Linn and Melanie and Jessica waved frantically at her. Phoebe made her way toward them.

"Excuse me, excuse me," she repeated as she bumped the knees of the people sitting. Finally, she reached her friends.

"Fee, you look beautiful!" Jessica exclaimed.

"It's just the skirt," Phoebe muttered, making sure it was on straight.

"Fee, this is so exciting!" Melanie squealed. "You were right—this *is* important! I even saw Mr. Hoffmann, from school!"

"The principal?"

Melanie nodded. "He told me he heard some people were trying to get books banned from the public library. And I told him *we* were going to do something about it. And you know what he said?"

"What?"

Melanie smiled smugly. "He said he was very proud of us."

Jessica jumped in. "And I told him *you* were our leader."

Phoebe didn't know what to say.

"Just think, Fee," Linn said, "after tonight you'll be famous!"

Phoebe gulped. Linn grabbed her arm. "And you know what else?"

Phoebe was afraid to ask. "What?"

Linn lowered her voice. "Chip didn't want me to

come. He said I'd look really nerdy if I got up in front of all these people."

"What did you say?"

Linn grinned proudly. "I told him I was a Doodlebug, and Doodlebugs stick together."

Phoebe resisted an urge to scream "You told him about the Doodlebugs?" This was no time to have a fight. She managed a thin grin. "Well, I'm glad you're here."

"Anyway, we sort of had a fight. Just a lovers' quarrel, really. And guess what? He's here!"

"Great." Phoebe just hoped he wouldn't boo. "I'd better get back to my seat."

Her three friends raised their hands simultaneously, displaying crossed fingers. "Good luck!"

Phoebe crossed her own fingers. "Same to you!"

She made her way back to the row where her parents and sisters were sitting. The room was quieting down and all eyes were on the five women and four men sitting at a long table in the front of the room. One of the women had a gavel in her hand and she rapped it on the table. Phoebe practically jumped out of her seat with each rap.

"This meeting of the Cedar Park Town Council will now come to order."

Phoebe took a deep breath. Okay, Fee, she told herself. This is it.

12

Now the room was silent. Phoebe wondered if everyone could hear her heart pounding under the thin white shirt. It definitely sounded loud enough to her. Those nine people sitting at the table looked like judges. Closing her eyes, Phoebe could picture them in long black robes, ready to pronounce sentence. Briefly, she wondered how many years she could get for trying to impersonate a grown-up.

The woman who held the gavel spoke. "We have a number of important issues to consider this evening, so we will get right to work. Councilman Perkins will introduce our first order of business."

A stocky, balding man with an intense expression rose.

"Madame Chairperson, council members, Cedar Park

residents: Our first item on the agenda is a highly controversial matter with serious ramifications that have far-reaching impact. Although the matter was only brought to my attention earlier this week, it is of such significance that I have requested the chairperson place it first on the agenda, to give it the highest priority."

Here we go, Phoebe thought. She twisted her hands together in her lap.

The man continued. "This is a matter of grave concern, a matter that affects our families, our lives, the very fabric of our existence." Little beads of sweat were forming on his head and his face was turning red. Phoebe held her breath.

"I am referring, of course, to the immediate and critical need for dog leash legislation."

Phoebe's breath came out in a whoosh and she promptly started coughing. Her mother turned to her with a look of concern.

"Are you all right?"

Phoebe couldn't speak for coughing and only managed to bob her head up and down. When she finished coughing, her eyes were all watery. On her other side, Daphne patted her hand.

"It's okay, Fee," her sister said comfortingly. "I mean, it's not as if we actually had a dog."

Phoebe nodded weakly and turned to see a petite, slender woman approaching the microphone set up in the aisle. She looked upset.

"Mr. Perkins!" Her amplified voice boomed out across the room, actually causing echoes. Phoebe gasped. Was that what *she* was going to sound like? The small woman also looked startled by the sound of her own voice. She jumped back from the mike.

"I moved to the suburbs so my poor sweet little poodle could run free! If I have to put her on a leash, I might as well have stayed in Chicago!" She looked like she was about to burst into tears as she backed away from the mike.

Another woman rose from the audience, not even bothering to go to the microphone. Her voice was loud enough on its own.

"Well, maybe it's your sweet little poodle that's been knocking over my garbage cans!"

Hearing this, the short woman ran back to the microphone. "Are you kidding?" she wailed. "My Fifi couldn't knock over an ashtray!"

"Can she dig up a garden?" another person yelled out.

The chairperson was rapping her gavel. "Please! We must have order!"

Phoebe watched the whole business with her mouth open. Was this what they called a town meeting? This was more like kindergarten. These people weren't even raising their hands!

The chairperson was eyeing the crowd nervously. "Obviously this is a highly emotional issue. There are other matters on the agenda which are less, uh, dramatic in nature. I suggest we table the dog leash discussion until we've finished voting on the other matters. All in favor?"

Nine council members' arms shot up immediately. Good, Phoebe thought. Now we can get on to the important stuff.

"The next item on the agenda demands our immediate attention, as it affects our children."

Phoebe sat up stiffly and smoothed the wrinkles on her skirt.

"We must decide tonight whether or not to begin extensive landscaping renovations in front of the high school."

Phoebe sank back in her chair.

At least the mention of landscaping didn't cause an uproar. Only one audience member had anything to say—something about kids needing trees—before the council voted.

Next came garbage maintenance. This created a little more of a stir. People lined up at the microphone to make suggestions as to methods of garbage collection.

"I never knew people took garbage so seriously," Phoebe whispered.

"Shhh," her mother murmured, but she punctuated it with a wink.

The garbage problem was resolved, and then it was time to discuss alternate side of the street parking. Once again, the lines formed at the microphones. Phoebe yawned. She took the paper from her pocket and looked at her speech, but she pretty much knew it by heart. Her mind wandered and she was only barely aware of the chairperson calling for a vote.

She was lost in a daydream when the words *public library* jerked her back to reality.

"According to several members of the community, there are books in the children's room they feel are totally inappropriate. On behalf of these parents, Mrs. Shirley Lane will present the issue."

Phoebe stiffened as she watched the plump, orange-haired woman rise from the audience and make her way to the microphone. She wore a bright turquoise pantsuit, a smug smile, and a general look of total confidence.

"Friends and fellow parents," she began. "I cannot begin to tell you how much it distresses me to talk about this shocking situation. But for the good of our community and the welfare of our children, I feel it is my ethical responsibility to bring this flagrant disregard for moral standards to your attention."

She paused and held up the book she was clutching.

"My youngest daughter Kimmie brought this book home from the library. It was written by a Betsy Drake, who, my daughter tells me, is a writer of children's books." She smiled sadly. "I feel it is more accurate to describe her as a writer of juvenile pornography."

A gasp went through the room. Phoebe leaned over and whispered to Lydia, "What's *pornography?*"

"Dirty books," Lydia whispered back.

Phoebe forced herself not to jump up and yell "They're not dirty!" She didn't want to sound like one of those dog leash people.

"Perhaps you think I am being a bit extreme in my assessment of this writer," Mrs. Lane continued. "As evidence, I will now read three passages from this book. I'm afraid many of you may find this offensive. I assure you that I am very uncomfortable in reading it to you." She opened the book and began to read.

*"Did you see Joanie in the locker room today?" I asked Sally.
"No. Why?"*

136

"She's got breasts! Big ones! I thought she was padding her bra. But she's not." I looked down at my own pathetic flat chest. "Do you think we'll ever grow big breasts like Joanie?"

Mrs. Lane paused dramatically, just long enough to give the council members a meaningful look. Then she flipped through some pages, and began reading again.

"Hey, Mom," I yelled excitedly. "Guess what? Guess what happened to me at school today?"

"I can't imagine. What happened?"

"I started menstruating! I got my period, right in the middle of class!"

"Darling, that's wonderful! You're a woman now!"

"It's a good thing you gave me that kit with the belt and the napkins. I knew exactly what to do!"

Mrs. Lane wrinkled her nose distastefully. "I'm sure you can see why I'm upset. To think that such personal and delicate matters would be written here for all to see is most distressing. If you'll bear with me, I'd like to read one more passage." She turned some pages and cleared her throat.

"Mom, can I ask you something personal?"

"Of course, dear."

"What does sex feel like? Does it hurt?"

Mrs. Lane stopped reading suddenly. "I'm afraid I can't even bring myself to continue with that passage. It's just too embarrassing. I'm sure you understand."

She closed the book and shook her head sorrowfully. "I have since discovered that there are eight other books by this so-called author on the shelves of the children's room at the Cedar Park Public Library. I have perused

137

these books and found to my horror that they all contain similar intimate references."

The chairperson broke in. "Mrs. Lane, exactly what are you recommending to the council?"

"I am recommending that all these Betsy Drake books be removed from the shelves of the children's room. I further recommend that a special parents' committee be established to examine other books in the collection to determine whether or not they're appropriate for our children."

One of the council members, looking distinctly puzzled, leaned forward and spoke.

"But isn't that the librarian's job?"

Phoebe turned around and looked at Ms. Wrenn. The librarian was staring straight ahead, her face expressionless.

Mrs. Lane was also looking at Ms. Wrenn. Then she turned back to the microphone.

"In all fairness, I am going under the assumption that Ms. Wrenn was not aware of the content of these books when she purchased them. Perhaps she is too busy to familiarize herself with every book in the collection. That is why I'm suggesting a parents' committee be established." She smiled modestly. "As you all know, I am a community leader and very busy myself. But I would be happy to organize and lead such a committee."

The council chairperson spoke. "Thank you, Mrs. Lane. Would anyone else like to address this issue?"

Phoebe smiled proudly as Ms. Wrenn rose. The pretty, well-dressed librarian made a sharp contrast to the woman who seemed reluctant to give up her place at the microphone. But as Ms. Wrenn approached, she did move aside.

"Good evening," Ms. Wrenn said in a calm, even voice. "As the children's librarian, I would like to take this opportunity to defend the selection and circulation of these books by Betsy Drake." She paused to consult some notes she had in her hand. "Ms. Drake is a highly regarded author who has won many children's book awards." She proceeded to recite the names of these awards. "Her books have been reviewed in all the major library and education publications. I will read to you from some of these reviews: '. . . a warm, witty, and realistic portrait of early adolescence. Obviously, Ms. Drake knows what young girls are thinking about and worried about, and she captures their feelings in language that young people will recognize. . . .'"

Ms. Wrenn went on to read other reviews that praised several Betsy Drake books. As she read, Phoebe was vaguely aware of the fact that her hands were cold. What if she froze and couldn't even get herself to the microphone? What if she got to the microphone but couldn't speak?

Ms. Wrenn finished reading. "These reviews testify as to the national recognition these books have received. On the basis of these reviews and my own professional qualifications in evaluating and selecting children's books, I believe these books are appropriate for young readers. Early adolescence is a time of confusion and young people need books like these to help them realize their problems and concerns are universal."

Phoebe was pleased to hear a smattering of applause when Ms. Wrenn finished talking. She was even happier when she realized two of the applauders were her own parents. But she felt a chill go through her when she heard the council chairperson say, "Would anyone else like to speak to this issue?"

Somehow, she willed herself to rise. Dimly, she knew her family's eyes were on her, and as she passed down the row, she felt Lydia's encouraging pat on her back. By the time she got into the aisle and made her way to the microphone, she knew everyone was watching her.

And then she was standing there, in front of the microphone. But the microphone was a good foot above her head.

A titter went through the audience and Phoebe felt her face going red. But a man sitting on the aisle jumped up and adjusted the microphone to fit her height.

"Thank you," Phoebe said politely, and then jumped as the words reverberated through the room. Again there was a titter.

Somehow, her hand found its way into her pocket and she drew out the paper. Maybe she knew it by heart, but the way she was feeling right that minute, she wasn't taking any chances.

Was her voice shaking? She couldn't tell.

"My name is Phoebe Gray. I'm eleven years old. I've read some of the Betsy Drake books, and I don't think there's anything wrong with them. Growing up isn't easy. Kids need books like these to help them grow up. Even if you don't like these books, you should not take them away from the library. Everybody likes different books, and nobody should have the right to tell other people what they can read. Now some of my friends will tell you more about these books." She turned slightly, and breathed a major sigh of relief when she saw the line that had formed behind her. She'd been so nervous she hadn't even heard them lining up.

She stepped aside and let Gina Allston have the mike. As Gina spoke, Phoebe floated back to her seat.

"Good work, pumpkin," her father whispered, and her mother blew a kiss. Her sisters, even Cassie, were beaming proudly at her. She sat down and let her body go limp. She'd done her part—now it was up to the others.

"These books help me understand all these strange things that are happening to me," Gina was saying. "And I think they should be in the library where kids like me can read them."

Leonard went next. "Some of you might think it's weird that a boy would read books like this. But my father told me it's important to understand how girls feel. I've learned a lot from these books."

Jessica talked about how she identified with some of the characters, and Melanie described how she had hated to read until she'd discovered the Betsy Drake books.

One by one, her classmates spoke. They all said pretty much the same things in different words—how much they liked the books, how the books helped them with their concerns, how they could relate to the characters. Phoebe looked at the council members to see how they

141

were reacting. One of them seemed to be doodling on a piece of paper. Another looked amused. But the others, including the chairperson, actually looked interested.

Linn was the last to speak. "My friend Phoebe said there are things that are more important than makeup and boyfriends, like being able to read what you want to read. At first I thought she was crazy. But maybe she's right. I don't think I want anyone telling me what I can read. I'm growing up, and I can choose my own books."

As Phoebe watched, Linn then turned from the mike and gazed directly at her mother sitting near the aisle looking startled. Phoebe couldn't hear what her friend said, but she could see Linn bat her eyelashes and could read her lips mouthing, "Okay, Mom?"

A slow smile appeared on Linn's mother's face and her lips said, "Maybe."

"Does anyone else have anything to say?" The chairperson looked like she hoped no one did. When there was no response, she was silent for a moment. And when she spoke again, her expression was troubled.

"I'm not sure what we should do at this point. After hearing Mrs. Lane, I was going to suggest that the council members read these books prior to voting on whether or not to recommend that the library remove them. But after hearing Ms. Wrenn and these young people speak so eloquently, I'm not sure if that's necessary."

Phoebe turned to Daphne. "What's *eloquently?*"

"Nicely," Daphne whispered back.

"After all," the chairperson continued, "aren't they the best judges?"

Mrs. Lane leaped up from her seat. "That's nonsense! They're only children!"

From the back of the room, there came a shout: "We are not!"

Phoebe saw a bearded man walking rapidly to the microphone. "Madame Chairperson, this is all very amusing, but I didn't come to this meeting to hear some little kids talking about their books. What I want to know is what we're going to do about getting the dogs leashed?"

And from the front of the room, a woman got up. "That's not fair! Just because a couple of wild dogs have been running around is no reason to force a leash on my collie!"

Then suddenly the whole room was buzzing and everyone was talking about dogs. Phoebe couldn't believe it. Here, the very freedom to read was at stake—and they were talking about stupid dog leashes!

The chairperson banged her gavel, but no one paid any attention. The room was in chaos. Barely aware of what she was doing, Phoebe pushed her way to the aisle and ran to the microphone.

"Hey, wait a minute!" she yelled, forgetting how strong the amplification was. The whole room went quiet and all eyes were on her. Phoebe didn't care. She was too angry.

"What's the matter with you guys? Do you care more about dogs than kids? This is really important! It's more important than any old dog leashes or garbage or anything else you've been talking about. Don't you realize this is about our rights—like, uh, like the right to eat fishburgers if that's what you want!"

Out of the corner of her eye Phoebe saw her parents turn to each other in surprise.

She pressed on. "No one says that you *have* to read Betsy Drake books—that's your choice—and how can you take that choice away? This isn't just a problem for kids. It's important to everybody, and I demand that you do something about it!"

Did she just say *demand*? Phoebe couldn't believe she'd been talking like that in front of a bunch of grown-ups.

But it worked. For the first time that evening, Phoebe saw a smile on the chairperson's face.

"Young lady, I think you're absolutely right." She turned to her colleagues. "We will now vote on Mrs. Lane's suggestion that we remove the books from the library. All in favor?"

Two council members tentatively raised their arms. Then, realizing no one else's were up, they quickly lowered them.

"All opposed?"

Seven hands shot up. The chairperson's eyes searched the room. They settled on Phoebe.

"Happy reading."

Phoebe was too stunned to say thank you.

Across the aisle, a red-faced Mrs. Lane was protesting vehemently. But the angry woman's voice was quickly drowned out by a roar of clapping and cheers.

"Madame Chairperson! Madame Chairperson!"

The man with the beard was at the microphone again.

"Yes?"

"Can we *please* talk about the leashes now?"

"That's quite a daughter you have there," Phoebe heard a woman say to her mother on the steps of Town Hall. Surrounded by her classmates, she couldn't hear her mother's response, but she felt pretty sure she knew what it was. Ms. Wrenn joined them, looking just as excited as the kids.

"Fee, that was beautiful! You told them exactly what they needed to hear. I'm very proud of you!"

Phoebe grinned happily. "We were all pretty mature, weren't we?" It was more a statement than a question. But she liked hearing Ms. Wrenn's response.

"Mature? Absolutely! That was a very mature presentation."

Then Leonard was standing before her. "Congratulations," he said formally. "You did very well."

"So did you!" Phoebe said.

"Fee!" Linn came dashing up and threw her arms around her. "That was great!"

Jessica and Melanie followed close behind. And then there was a whole crowd around her, congratulating her and telling her how well she had done. Phoebe was grinning so hard her jaw was hurting.

Then a reporter from her father's newspaper came up wanting a picture of all the kids involved, with Ms. Wrenn. Phoebe moved where he told her to. She felt like she was floating on air.

The crowd started to thin out. "C'mon, Ms. Celebrity, we're leaving," her father said, steering her out of the crowd. While the rest of the family walked, Phoebe skipped to the car.

"You did good, kid," Lydia said. "For a fledgling revolutionary."

"I thought you were wonderful," Daphne added.

Even Cassie was enthusiastic. "I heard this real cute guy say you were a neat kid. When I told him I was your sister, he was definitely impressed." She paused thoughtfully. "I wonder if he's got a girlfriend. . . ."

"I think this calls for a celebration," Mr. Gray announced as they all got in the station wagon. "I suggest we toast our Phoebe with ice cream sundaes."

"Sounds good to me," Mrs. Gray said. "How does that sound to you girls?"

A chorus of general approval greeted this. Phoebe bounced up and down. "I'm going to have *three* scoops, with hot fudge and whipped cream and chopped nuts—"

"Oh, Fee," Cassie said reprovingly. "Grow up."

But this time those words didn't bother Phoebe at all. She kept on bouncing and her smile just got broader. Because she *was* growing up. In her very own way.

Some more titles in Lions Teen Tracks:

- ☐ **Tell Me If the Lovers are Losers** *Cynthia Voigt* £2.25
- ☐ **In Summer Light** *Zibby Oneal* £1.95
- ☐ **Happy Endings** *Adèle Geras* £2.25
- ☐ **Strictly for Laughs** *Ellen Conford* £1.95
- ☐ **The Warriors of Taan** *Louise Lawrence* £2.25
- ☐ **Second Star to the Right** *Deborah Hautzig* £1.95

All these books are available at your local bookshop or newsagent, or to order direct from the publishers, just tick the titles you want and fill in the form below.

NAME (Block letters) _____

ADDRESS _____

_____

Send to: Collins Childrens Cash Sales, PO Box 11, Falmouth, Cornwall, TR10 9EP

I enclose a cheque or postal order or debit my Visa/Mastercard to the value of the cover price plus:

UK: 60p for the first book, 25p for the second book, plus 15p per copy for each additional book ordered to a maximum charge of £1.90.

BFPO: 60p for the first book, 25p for the second book plus 15p per copy for the next 7 books, thereafter 9p per book

Overseas and Eire: £1.25 for the first book, 75p for the second book, thereafter 28p per book.

Credit card no: _____

Expiry Date: _____

Signature: _____

Lions reserve the right to show new retail prices on covers which may differ from those previously advertised in the text or elsewhere.

Some more titles in Lions Teen Tracks:

☐ **Catch You On the Flipside** *Pete Johnson* £1.95
☐ **The Chocolate War** *Robert Cormier* £2.25
☐ **Rumble Fish** *S E Hinton* £1.95
☐ **Tex** *S E Hinton* £1.95
☐ **Breaking Up** *Frank Willmott* £1.95

Some more titles in Lions Teen Tracks:

☐ **Slambash Wangs of a Compo Gormer**
   Robert Leeson £2.50
☐ **The Bumblebee Flies Anyway** *Robert Cormier* £1.95
☐ **After the First Death** *Robert Cormier* £2.25
☐ **That Was Then, This Is Now** *S E Hinton* £1.95
☐ **Centre Line** *Joyce Sweeney* £2.25

All these books are available at your local bookshop or newsagent, or to order direct from the publishers; just tick the titles you want and fill in the form below.

NAME (Block letters) _____

ADDRESS _____

_____

Send to: Collins Childrens Cash Sales, PO Box 11, Falmouth, Cornwall, TR10 9EP

I enclose a cheque or postal order or debit my Visa/Mastercard to the value of the cover price plus:

UK: 60p for the first book, 25p for the second book, plus 15p per copy for each additional book ordered to a maximum charge of £1.90.

BFPO: 60p for the first book, 25p for the second book plus 15p per copy for the next 7 books, thereafter 9p per book

Overseas and Eire: £1.25 for the first book, 75p for the second book, thereafter 28p per book.

Credit card no: _____

Expiry Date: _____

Signature: _____

Lions reserve the right to show new retail prices on covers which may differ from those previously advertised in the text or elsewhere.

Some more titles in Lions Teen Tracks:

☐ **Come a Stranger** *Cynthia Voigt* £2.25
☐ **Waiting for the Sky to Fall** *Jacqueline Wilson* £1.95
☐ **A Formal Feeling** *Zibby Oneal* £1.95
☐ **If This is Love, I'll Take Spaghetti** *Ellen Conford* £1.95
☐ **Moonwind** *Louise Lawrence* £1.95

All these books are available at your local bookshop or newsagent, or to order direct from the publishers, just tick the titles you want and fill in the form below.

NAME (Block letters) _____

ADDRESS _____

_____

Send to: Collins Childrens Cash Sales, PO Box 11, Falmouth, Cornwall, TR10 9EP

I enclose a cheque or postal order or debit my Visa/Mastercard to the value of the cover price plus:

UK: 60p for the first book, 25p for the second book, plus 15p per copy for each additional book ordered to a maximum charge of £1.90.

BFPO: 60p for the first book, 25p for the second book plus 15p per copy for the next 7 books, thereafter 9p per book

Overseas and Eire: £1.25 for the first book, 75p for the second book, thereafter 28p per book.

Credit card no: _____

Expiry Date: _____

Signature: _____

Lions reserve the right to show new retail prices on covers which may differ from those previously advertised in the text or elsewhere.